THE SEAMSTRESS ON CIDER LANE
Homefront Hearts #2

Jillianne Hamilton writes delightful historical fiction and historical romance featuring rebellious women and happy endings. Her debut novel was shortlisted for the PEI Book Award and her debut historical fiction novel was longlisted for the Historical Fiction Company Book Award. She lives in Charlottetown on Canada's east coast.

OTHER BOOKS BY THE AUTHOR

The Hobby Shop on Barnaby Street
The Land Girl on Lily Road

The Spirited Mrs. Pringle

The Lazy Historian's Guide to the Wives
of Henry VIII

Molly Miranda: Thief for Hire
Molly Miranda: Thick as Thieves
Molly Miranda: Honor Among Thieves

the Seamstress *on* Cider Lane

A HOMEFRONT HEARTS NOVEL

TFP

prologue

Nora

—⋇—

I knew Jack's type right away—too handsome and too charming for his own good, an easy smile that he shared with everyone, and a countenance that made all the girls feel special, like they were the only one in the room.

I was onto him immediately.

"Do I know you from somewhere?"

"Do you?" My eyes narrowed. "Maybe?"

He studied my face and sat back a little. "I've definitely seen you before."

I gave a little shrug. "Maybe I just have one of those faces."

"I assure you, you do not." He raised his brows so I would understand that he meant it as a compliment.

I fought the urge to roll my eyes.

"Where are you from? Maybe we have friends in common." Jack finished his pint.

"Deptford."

His mouth tightened as he considered this. "No, that's not it."

This did not surprise me. His posh accent and jumper hinted at a chap who didn't travel south of the Thames very often.

Jack, giving up for the moment, offered to buy us drinks, and within a few minutes the four of us were squeezing onto the dance floor as Glenn Miller's "Moonlight Serenade" played on the wireless.

As Jack and I swayed to the melody, I watched Maisie and Cal, their forms moving closer together.

"You know," Jack said, lowering his mouth to my ear, "you don't have to babysit your friend."

"I'm not," I said, turning my head quickly towards him, inadvertently brushing the tip of my nose against the stubble on his high cheekbone.

Jack's olive green eyes met mine for a moment and he smiled serenely as he straightened.

Over his shoulder I noticed the clock on the wall above the bar.

"I should get going," I whispered. "The siren—"

"You're not even going to wait until the song is over?"

"My landlord likes to lock the Andie if we're tardy."

"She sounds a right gem," he said. "Perhaps I can walk you home? That way you don't have to interrupt them." He nodded to Maisie and Cal who seemed like they were in their own little world.

I sighed and dropped my hand from his shoulder. "Fine."

Out on the pavement, I pulled my torch from my bag and gave it a gentle thump against my side to get the thing to glow.

"You really ought to get some new batteries for that," Jack suggested unhelpfully.

"The batteries are fine," I said. "The torch is just useless unless you get a little rough with it, that's all."

As if on queue the blasted thing went out, plunging us into darkness. "Bollocks."

"I think you may have been a little *too* rough with it."

I glared up at him, or at least the dark figure that I was fairly confident was him.

Giving the torch a few more slaps with my palm, I grumbled at it and tossed it back in my bag.

"Where do you live?"

"Barnaby Street, near Covent Garden."

"Right," he said, sounding confident. "This way."

We chatted as we walked. He asked me what I did for work, how I knew Maisie and if I expected anything to happen between Maisie and Cal. I learned how he knew Cal and Francis and he told me why the three of them gathered at the pub that night—to mourn the loss of Francis' cousin and a friend of Jack's.

"It's probably a good thing you two passed by the windows," he said, smiling weakly. "We probably would have ended up drowning our sorrows a little too enthusiastically."

"I'm so sorry for your loss." I shook my head. "That's terrible. Nobody should have to deal with such a thing. This bloody war is so stupid and horrible." I squeezed his hand. "Tell me about your friend."

"We met at Cambridge. He was brilliant."

Ah. So he is posh. I knew it.

He was quiet after that and I didn't wish to prod him further.

"It's awfully hard to figure out how I recognize you when I can't even see you," Jack said after a few minutes of silence between us.

"You may just have to live the rest of your life wondering."

"I'm going to figure it out. I might just have to…take you out to dinner so I have more time to think about it."

I stopped as a nearby cab splashed light across his grinning face for a split second, highlighting the ginger in his neatly cut blond hair.

"How many times have you used that line before?"

"What?"

"Tell me. I'd like to know."

"What play?"

I dropped my voice slightly to mock him. "Oh, you look *so* familiar. I simply *must* take you to dinner so I can figure out where I've seen you before." I crossed my arms over my chest. "It's a bit much."

"I promise it's not a trick," he laughed.

We stood in front of a pub, the lights from inside leaking out between the gaps in their blackout curtains, illuminating the sign over the door just enough for me to read it. It was a name I didn't recognize.

"Bloody hell," I said. "Where are we?"

"I'm…not sure." Jack looked around for street markers but the two closest signs were draped in the black of night.

I scanned the street up and down for a cab but things were so quiet.

I exhaled loudly. "I can't even believe this."

The sound I had been dreading rose slowly, growing louder and louder—the air raid siren. Locals soon poured out of the pub and nearby homes, heading to their closest shelters. In this case, it was the Blackfriars tube station. Jack pointed to the signage as we followed the flood of people.

We found an empty space on the train platform and slid down to sit on the cold floor. I couldn't even imagine spending every night down in a place like this rather than in my bunk in Mrs. Martin's Anderson shelter.

"How did we even end up here?"

Jack nudged me with his shoulder. "Probably because we were so distracted by our witty banter and sparkling conversation."

"I think you somehow sabotaged my flashlight."

"Oh?" He smirked. "And how exactly did I manage—"

His question was interrupted by a stream of low rumbles, pops, and booms from above. Lamps shuddered, blinked out and flickered back on, dimming off and on for the next hour as the Luftwaffe performed their nightly assault on London yet again.

"Are you planning to stay in London, even with all this?" Jack nodded at the curved ceiling of the tube station.

"Leave? And let the Nazis know that I'm scared of them? Never."

The corner of Jack's mouth tugged into a reluctant smile.

"Besides, I don't have anywhere to go." I shrugged.

I wanted to ask him why he was still in London and not serving on some military base but figured it was none of my business.

My ears must have numbed to the sounds of destruction and chaos—enough, anyway, for me to fall asleep at some point. When I woke to the sound of the all clear siren I bolted upright, not knowing where I was at first. I only relaxed slightly when I realized I was cuddled up tight against Jack, his jacket over my shoulders. I'd left a slight damp spot on the front of his shirt.

From drooling on him in my sleep.

I groaned and quickly wiped at the corners of my mouth, trying my best not to smear my red lipstick any worse than it already was.

"I'm so sorry." I slid off his jacket and shoved it at him. "I believe this is yours."

"It's quite alright," he said, bracing his hand against the wall as he stood.

Struggling to my feet I slipped my shoes back on, thankful they weren't stolen while I slept. I grabbed my compact out of my bag—it, too, having survived the night—and winced as I surveyed my messy strawberry blonde hair, every piece of it seeming to stick out at a different angle.

There was nothing for it. I would have to walk back to Barnaby Street looking like I stuck my finger in an outlet. I groaned again and threw my compact back in my bag.

"It's not that bad," Jack assured me, sliding his arms into his jacket. "I'm sure my hair is far messier than yours."

I flicked him a glance. His hair remained tidy and his clothes still somehow looked freshly ironed. He didn't even have shadows under his eyes, the blighter.

He didn't need to know that though.

"I better walk you home," he said as we joined the queue forming to leave the tube station shelter.

"Because that worked so well the last time you tried it?"

"It wasn't so bad, was it?"

I gave him a meaningful look.

The rising sun drenched the overcast sky in an orange radiance, giving every dark purple cloud a vibrant glow. The streets filled with slow-moving pedestrians, all emerging from overnight hideaways.

After a few blocks of silence Jack stopped, gesturing to a different street. "I'm going this way."

"Ah. Farewell then." I gave a limp flourish with my hand.

"Wait," he said, a mischievous gleam in his eyes. "I, uh, think you should give me your address. When I finally remember where I've seen you before, I can write to you and let you know."

"I still don't believe you." I chuckled.

"And perhaps," he added, "I could take you out for dinner sometime."

I raised an eyebrow at him. "Just to be clear, you saw the puddle on your shirt this morning and you thought to yourself, 'I want to take this bird out for a meal.'"

He laughed heartily. "It wasn't the drool specifically—"

"The manic hair then?" When he didn't reply, I stepped closer to him. "You know, you're supposed to take a girl out *before* you sleep with her." My lips curled into a smile as I waited for his shocked response.

None came. Instead, he simply smiled and said, "I'm unconventional."

Yes, Jack, you are.

I was intrigued. But I'd learned from my mistakes long ago. I pulled a pen and a receipt from my bag, scribbling the hobby shop address on it.

"When you figure out how you recognized me, let me know." I handed him the receipt. "And then…"

"And then?"

"And then maybe I'll let you take me out."

Jack nodded, seemingly satisfied with that response. I hadn't expected that.

A lot of blokes wouldn't bother with a woman who made them jump through so many hoops, especially when he was Mr. Perfect and London was full of young and pretty single gals with few young men to choose from.

"I promise I'll figure it out." He tucked the receipt into his pocket. "Have a good day, Nora. I'll be seeing you soon."

As I walked back to Barnaby Street, I sighed to myself. I had to admit spending the night cradled in the arms of a handsome chap wasn't the worst way to spend the night during a raid.

Too bad I'll never hear from him again.

one

Nora

———❧———

"I've had it!" Victoria's long and elegant fingers curled into fists at her sides, her jaw set. She swiped furiously at the tear running down her cheek and sniffed. "I can't take it anymore."

"I'm so sorry," I murmured.

I didn't know what else to say. All I could do was stare wide-eyed at the smoldering wreckage before us. A few blackened beams still stood. The sewing desk where I spent countless hours, stitching beautiful garments until my shoulders ached, was a pile of ash. My gorgeous Singer sewing machine lay on the floor, burnt and partially melted by the angry flames. The front counter where Victoria met with clients and the shelves where we stored our fabric bolts were simply gone.

The metallic silhouettes of four dress forms remained—the only witnesses to the devastating fire from the night before.

The Germans bombed the building I lived in *and* the shop where I worked. I was beginning to take it personally.

There were several bombing raids the month before that nearly made my resolve crack. London was under attack for over eight hours. Twelve hundred people died on that one horrible night alone.

The raid that took out the tailoring shop was somehow even more severe. It was like the Germans bombs were so constant, the entire world shuddered and roared.

I looked over my shoulder, surveying the damage the fire had taken. About half the street was reduced to ash. A few families and business owners slowly approached the smoking remains, staring blankly, cursing the Nazis or sobbing. There was no looks of shock though, only overwhelm and despair.

Victoria let out a long unsteady breath. "Well, that's it then. I have to leave London. My sister has invited me to live with her just outside Leeds. My daughter is living with her."

I nodded stiffly. "Probably for the best."

"You should leave London too." She cleared her throat, keeping her emotions at bay. "The raids are worse than ever. They could get even worse."

I straightened my shoulders. "Unless those bastards arrive on English soil, I'm staying right here."

I already made the sacrifice of moving out of central London. The Nazis would have to try harder to get me to leave the city entirely.

The journey back to north London was long. I'd left the house early that morning because I knew the trains and buses would be delayed because of bomb damage, only to find I no longer had a job to attend to. Exhausted by all of it, I leaned my head against the window as the bus inched along an undisturbed stretch of road, struggling to move as too many vehicles squeezed onto a single street.

I could hear shouting outside the bus—a man yelling at a bobby, asking him when he would have access to the water and gas lines again. It seemed like most of the city was without utilities that morning.

I used up all my best profanity on cursing the Nazis months ago. Now all I could do was wait and hope to see the day when the stupid war would end.

After having a late morning self-pitying nap, I joined my aunt Gloria down in the living room. She glanced up from her newspaper before lowering it to her lap.

"You startled me, dear." She slapped a hand to her chest. "I didn't know you were home. Is everything alright?"

I flopped down into the floral patterned armchair across from her, swinging my legs over one arm and lounging sideways. "I have to find another job. The shop burned down last night."

"Oh, sweetheart. I'm sorry to hear that." She folded the newspaper and set it aside. "With so many people leaving London, I'm sure you could find another job somewhere else doing the same type of work."

If I was living with anyone else, they might have been concerned about my sudden lack of employment. However, Aunt Gloria and her husband Harry lived in a lovely house on a lovely street in a lovely neighborhood and didn't need to charge me rent. In fact, they insisted I save my money since I was family.

Even after six months of living with them, I still wasn't exactly sure what Uncle Harry did for a job—some sort of business consulting. I only knew they lived comfortably enough to afford the charming and spacious Victorian in Highgate and taking me in was not much of a financial burden. I also understood that Gloria and my mother—twins who were, at one time, very much alike in looks *and* personality—had gone on to lead very different lives after marriage. Gloria's accent even changed to match that of her posh Oxford-educated husband, leaving behind her estuary accent.

"I would offer to make you some tea but the water and gas are still off." Gloria frowned. Her eyes lingered on the newspaper on the couch beside her. "Maybe you could enlist and focus on that for a while until things calm down. They're always begging for more women workers in the newspaper." She rolled her eyes and crossed her arms over her chest. "As if we women don't have enough to worry about without having to go into factories to make bombs and bullets."

I hoped to avoid conscription; those in the garment design industry were exempt from war work. If I didn't find a replacement job right away, I would be forced into taking nurse's training or—even worse— chopping trees down in the country.

I snatched the newspaper from the couch and flipped to the job listings, my eyes flicking from one listing to another.

"Oh, joy," I muttered. "I could operate a lift or work on a bus."

"Don't be a snob. Every job is an important job right now."

I frowned at her. "Would *you* want to be a train conductor?"

"Me? Of course not." Her plump blonde curls bounced as she chuckled.

"Fact is I'm very good at sewing and rubbish at most other things." I continued to review the job adverts, quickly becoming more and more disheartened.

"We both know that's not true." Aunt Gloria drummed her fingertips on the arm of the couch. "You know, you could always open your own shop."

I lowered the newspaper and waited for her to laugh at her own joke. She didn't.

"I can't afford that," I said.

"You must have *some* money saved up."

She was right. Not having to pay rent for six months helped me save and I still had a most of the cash I earned with Maisie when we briefly did portrait photography together. However, it was not nearly enough. When I looked into opening my own shop before, the list of start-up expenses made my head spin, and there wasn't even a war on then. I needed a new sewing machine—a good one. Fabric was becoming more expensive as shortages affected almost everything. Retail space was at a premium after bombs destroyed dozens of shopfronts in a single night. Although the raids were no longer every night by then, we had still lived through it for eight months.

Gloria's brown eyes flitted around her carefully curated living room decor. She did this a lot. When one grows up poor and suddenly has access to money, the urge to surround oneself with nice things is undeniable—fine furniture, pretty floral curtains, a German-made cuckoo clock, and far too many framed photos of her darling son.

She finally sat back on the sofa and let her gaze wander back to me. "What if I loaned you the money?"

I shook my head while my hands did an odd flailing motion of their own volition. "No, no, no. You have done so much for me already. I could never ask that of you—"

"You're not asking, dear. I'm offering—"

"I couldn't—"

"You can!"

"I can't take any more from you. You already let me live here for free—"

"Nonsense. We enjoy having you here with us."

"Perhaps I can get a small business loan instead—"

"Which will come with interest. Don't be silly. Give me a number and I'll talk it over with Harry this evening. I'm sure he won't have a problem with loaning you the money." Gloria arched a brow at me. "See? Just that simple."

"You're not going to let me decline, are you?"

She let out a little laugh. "No. It's already settled."

I fell back into the armchair, suddenly overwhelmed and exhausted all over again.

Welcome to the world, Archer Fashion & Tailoring.

two

JACK

———✦———

That day in late May began with the scrambling of tiny clawed feet scurrying up the length of my body.

My eyes flashed open and I flung the quilt off, leaping to my feet. As my pulse raced, I scanned the lumpy couch I slept on nightly. A long pink tail disappeared between the cushions and I shuddered at the sight of the uninvited and very unappreciated guest. I lifted the cushion and groaned loudly as the little white mouse then squeezed through a small rip, mouse droppings dotting the fabric.

Francis, my friend and flatmate at the time, continued sleeping in his nearby bedroom, snoring so loudly that I wondered if the neighbors could hear him. I knew it was wrong to complain, given that Francis offered me his couch after my flat was bombed several weeks before, but I was so tired. Always *so* tired. The combination of the hard, uneven cushions, the regular trips down to the nearby shelter for a good portion of the night, and the long train ride to my job was all taking its toll on me.

I arrived at Highgate Grammar School fifteen minutes late that day despite the early morning mouse wake-up call. My pupils, a mix of Year

One boys and girls in green and gold uniforms, all chatted and laughed within their friend groups while a few others threw paper airplanes at one another. Several of them turned to look at me as I entered the classroom, but only three returned to their seats, the rest not terribly concerned that their teacher was at his desk, glaring at them.

"Children, please take your seats," I said, using my best 'listen to me or else' voice I inherited from my stepfather somehow. "Children? Children, please can you please take your seats?"

One of the overly keen girls near the front raised her hand but didn't wait for me to answer it before speaking. "Mr. Parker, why are you late?"

"I fell asleep on the train and missed my stop," I mumbled, too tired to lie. I cleared my throat and addressed the class again. "I asked you to take your seats." It was like they couldn't hear me.

A sore spot in my back gave me a painful pinch as I stood again and slapped my palms on the desktop. "I said sit down!"

All of these kids already hate you. Only bad teachers need to shout at children.

I cleared my throat again as they finally all slid behind their desks, none of them looking particularly daunted by my raised voice.

"Without opening your books, who remembers the Roman power pyramid we discussed yesterday?" I sat back down. "Who can tell me the names of the people directly under the emperor?"

I answered a raised hand.

"Senators and patricians," a boy called Marvin said.

"Very good. And the level below that? Anyone else?"

I selected a girl near the front.

"Equestrians," she responded confidently.

One of the boys at the back of the class, Anthony, made a neighing sound while his chums nearby laughed. I rolled my eyes and shook my head at him.

Just then I noticed a few of the boys glancing down at Anthony's open satchel, glancing at me and then back at the bag. I assumed it was a frog again or maybe a kitten like a few months ago.

I released an exasperated sigh. "Anthony, what's in your bag this time?"

"Nothing."

"Bring your satchel up here please."

His friend let slip a snort of laughter before whispering to Anthony. Grinning, Anthony slid his hand under the strap of his bag and slowly brought it to my desk. He shifted it onto my desk and ran back to his desk, his friends giggling again at the back of the room.

I lifted the top flap of the bag and my eyes immediately widened. My chair screeched along the floor as I slid it backwards and bolted to my feet, the urge to vomit washing over me.

An unexploded incendiary bomb lay peacefully inside, tucked in between his lunchbox and his books. Several children had already died in Britain after finding unexploded bombs and using them like toys. Anthony evidently wanted to join them.

"Everyone, please evacuate to the flagpole in front of the school. Stay in a quiet and orderly line while I deal with this," I ordered, moving in front of the desk and waving the children by.

Anthony sauntered by, still smirking wickedly, and I considered sticking my foot out as he walked. It wasn't the first time the thought had crossed my mind.

I always looked forward to the bell at the end of the school day but on that particular day, the bell couldn't sound soon enough. As I took my usual route back to the train station, my satchel in hand, I heard someone calling my name.

"Mr. Parker!" Marvin hurried after me, his bicycle at his side. "What happened with the bomb?"

I had finished the class outside on the green in front of the school while the authorities came to collect the explosive.

"All taken care of," I said. "We can go back to the classroom tomorrow."

He nodded.

Marvin was one of my more tolerable students—intelligent and thoughtful. I had tutored him the term before when he was trying to catch up with his classmates after having just returned from the country. More and more children filtered back to London every day despite the government not yet giving the all clear to do so.

"I was also wondering…are you alright?"

I chuckled. "What?"

"That is, I mean no disrespect, sir, but you look bloody awful."

"Language!" I snapped, pretending to be offended when I was actually quite touched that he noticed and thought to ask.

"Sorry," he added quickly.

I sighed. "My living situation is…not ideal at the moment. My old flat was bombed a few weeks ago and I'm staying at my mate's place. I shouldn't be telling you this."

Marvin blinked up at me. "Why don't you rent our garret?"

"That's very kind—"

"I know Mum would rather rent to you rather than another bombee she doesn't know," he added, speaking quickly.

The house is close to the school. And I wouldn't have to sleep on a rodent-infested couch. And his mother is a good cook…

"Thank you very much for the offer, Marvin, but it's likely inappropriate for a teacher to live in the same house as a—"

"I'll go ask my mum right now. I'm sure she'll say yes. Bye, Mr. Parker!" Marvin was already pedalling away down the pavement.

When the kitchen light flicked on in the flat the next morning, my exhausted eyes tried to focus as I slowly summoned the gumption to wake up. The blurry figure moved around the kitchen, busying itself making tea. As the fuzzy image took shape, I froze. It was a woman in her knickers.

She must have sensed me watching her because she suddenly looked over her shoulder at me, shrieked, slapped her hands over her chest and scurried back to the bedroom.

Francis appeared in the bedroom doorway, howling with laughter.

"Stop it," I heard her snap. "Who the bloody hell is *that*?!"

"My mate, Jack." Francis grinned. "His flat was bombed so he's sleepin' here."

"And you never thought to mention that last night?"

Francis bit his lip, attempting to smother his chuckles.

"I'm sorry if I startled you," I called into the bedroom, wincing.

"He saw me in my *knickers*," she whisper-hissed.

Francis shrugged and headed for the kitchen. "It's nothing he hasn't seen before."

I shook my head at him, my eyes bulging, mouthing, "Are you mad?"

The woman marched out of the bedroom, her khaki green ATS uniform looking a bit rumpled, and she headed for the door. "I can't believe I fell for your shenanigans again. I am such a fool!" She slammed the door on her way out of the flat.

Francis shrugged again. "She'll be back."

Marvin handed me the bowl of steaming mashed potatoes from across the dinner table that night. I'm not sure what Mrs. Sampson put in her potatoes but they were heavenly. The large and spotless dining room was bright and smelled amazing as all the scents of food mingled in the air above the crowded tabletop.

"I'm grateful for the invitation to move to your upstairs garret," I said, scooping some onto my plate. "But like I told Marvin yesterday, it might be a bit awkward—a teacher living in the same house as a student."

"I promise I won't bother you," Marvin said, his soft brown eyes widening.

I smiled. "I didn't mean it like that."

Mrs. Sampson sipped from her water glass. "It's no trouble at all. You can't stay where you're at now."

"Besides," Mr. Sampson added with a firm nod, "there's a war on. A lot of people are living in places they wouldn't have chosen otherwise." His thin dark hair was slicked back in a deep widow's peak and his bushy brows seemed permanently furrowed.

"And we're so close to the school," his wife added.

"True," I said. "I wouldn't miss that long train ride every morning, that's for certain."

Taking a mouthful of the carrots on my plate, I let the sweet, buttery taste melt in my mouth for a moment. After eating like a bachelor for a couple years, the taste of those vegetables was something akin to a religious experience.

"You won't have to worry about me as a tenant," I said. "All I do is mark assignments and read in the evenings."

"It's settled then. You can move your things in upstairs whenever you like." Mrs. Sampson beamed.

Before I could express my gratitude, Mr. Sampson cut in.

"What were you doing before the war? Something at Cambridge?"

A pang of longing needled my stomach. "Yes, that's correct. Research. I did a lot of work with deciphering documents from the seventeenth and eighteenth centuries mostly. Some assistant teaching work as well."

"And now you teach history at our school," Marvin joined in. "Why?"

I smiled weakly. Marvin didn't need to know how much I hated teaching his class—almost as much as I hated that he was even back in London and not still safe in the country in the first place.

"When me and every other young man enlisted for the war effort, the schools lost quite a few young teachers and since I was educated, the powers that be decided I would do a satisfactory job teaching history."

Marvin blinked up at me, tilting his blond head. "So, you actually did join up?"

"I did. This is how I am serving in the war effort, I suppose."

"Everyone is doing their bit in different ways," Mrs. Sampson said, her voice comforting.

Marvin sat back in his chair. "Anthony said you must have got the job because you're a conchie but I told him that wasn't true."

Anthony. That little brat.

"Don't listen to anything Anthony says. He just likes telling tales and starting trouble," Mrs. Sampson warned. "I can't believe he brought a bomb to class."

"What do you think of those conchies?" Mr. Sampson gestured to me with his fork. "What do you think they're trying to prove?"

That war is a pointless and bloody game where men in power hide away in their keeps, safe from the guns and the bombs, while millions of young men are sent to fight and die for no reason.

Mr. Sampson wasn't actually looking for my opinion on conscientious objectors. He just wanted to make sure I wasn't one of them.

I hesitated. "They're selfish. England can use all the manpower it can get and these chaps choose to not join the fight. It's amoral."

Mr. Sampson nodded. "Quite right."

I sensed myself tensing slightly. I couldn't voice my actual opinion on the matter. Not only could I lose my new residence but I could also lose my job.

Shortly after, I bid the Sampson family a good night and had to dash, realizing I might miss the last train back. As I took the corner to the home's foyer, I noticed a wall of framed family photos and my gaze instantly landed on one familiar face.

It was Nora.

I knew I'd seen her before.

In the photo, she had her arm around Marvin's shoulder, pulling him tight to her. I realized they must be related somehow—cousins maybe?

Everything from the night we met came rushing back to me— her cheeky remarks, the mischievous look in her eyes, her wit, her confidence, her smile. On the night we met, I recognized her from somewhere but she didn't believe me. I must have seen the photo when I tutored Marvin. I wrote to her but she never responded to any of my letters.

Suddenly remembering I had a train to catch I returned back to earth, rounding the corner to the front door.

In a split second, I was on all fours in the Sampson's foyer. My palms burned from the impact with the carpet. Several fabric rolls pooled around me. I looked behind me where a blonde woman sat up from the floor and inspected her arm for injuries.

"I'm so sorry!" I exclaimed, getting to my feet. "Are you alright? I was rushing out the door and didn't even hear you—"

"It's my fault," she laughed. "I couldn't see where I was going and—" She looked at me over her shoulder and her eyes softened. "Oh. Hello, Jack."

My heart skipped a beat.

"Hello, Nora."

<h1 style="text-align:center">three</h1>

Nora

———✦———

I hadn't expected to see Jack ever again. So naturally when I finally did, I ended up running into him—literally—when my arms were full of supplies for the shop.

After we picked ourselves up from the floor, we shared an awkward little laugh.

"You're lucky I was running in with cloth and not fabric shears," I said, dusting some debris off a bolt of cotton and leaning it up against the wall.

Gloria appeared around the corner. "Oh, Nora. You're home. I see you've met our new tenant."

I blinked at her and then glanced at Jack. "Tenant?"

The corner of his mouth quirked up uneasily. "Indeed."

"We've actually met before," I threw in, even though Gloria hadn't asked. "We, uh, have a couple friends in common."

Gloria beamed. "Oh, lovely!"

Jack glanced down at his watch. "I'm so sorry. I have to run. My train—"

"I'll go with you," I blurted, "to the station, I mean." I winced, realizing I likely sounded ridiculously eager. "We can catch up."

His eyes lit up. "Uh, sure." He opened the door for me and waved me through.

Once we were outside and walking to the station, neither of us spoke right away. I repeatedly glanced at him, hoping he'd say something so I wouldn't have to.

"So," he finally said, "Marvin is your…cousin?"

"Yes. Gloria is my mum's twin sister," I said. "I've lived with them for about six months."

A flicker of realization appeared on Jack's face and he glanced down at me. "Why did you leave your flat on Barnaby Street?"

"It didn't seem like the best place for me to live after it got blown up."

"Ah. Yes, well, that makes sense." His jaw tensed for a moment. "So, you didn't receive any of my letters then?"

"Oh." My stomach fluttered. "No. I'm sorry, I didn't. They didn't make it to my old post office either."

His olive green eyes warmed. "Here I thought you just ignored me." He stopped walking as we neared the train station.

"No, of course not." I chuckled. "Does that mean you figured out how you recognized me after all?"

"You remember." His voice was quiet, his smile thoughtful. "And no, I didn't until I saw your photo at their house. I must have seen it before when I tutored Marvin. So, I cheated and wrote to you anyway. I just…" He released a breath. "I hoped to see you again."

I wanted to see you too.

His thick dark blonde hair looked almost white, catching the light of the evening sun. It glinted off his blonde whiskers that peppered his strong jaw and high cheekbones.

"Well, we'll be seeing each other every day now," I said, swallowing, "since we'll be living in the same house soon."

"Yes. Right." A look of dread passed over his face. "What are the chances?"

I swallowed. "This war has brought lots of people together unexpectedly."

"I better go," he said quietly, his eyes not quite meeting mine.

"Good night, Nora."

"Bye, Jack." I nodded at him as he headed for the platform.

As I walked home, Jack's disappointed expression stuck in my mind. He obviously realized he couldn't take me out while we lived under the same roof, particularly when that roof belonged to my aunt and uncle. Surely he knew that.

Not that he would have any serious interest in me anyway.

It had been months since we'd seen one another and we had only spent a few hours together that night.

And it's not like I would necessarily agree to go out with him even if he asked me.

He still seemed far too posh and perfect for my taste anyway. Really, he wasn't my type at all and I knew that. I *knew* that. I knew that, and yet I felt the need to repeat it over and over in my head as I climbed the stairs to my little bedroom on the first floor.

"Could use a bit o' paint," said Mr. Culpepper the next day from the doorway of his cobbler shop across the street. He cleared his throat loudly, adding, "Definitely needs to be repainted. T'would make it look much nicer."

Throwing him a weak smile over my shoulder, I continued struggling to unlock my shop's front door while also cradling three bolts of fabric under one arm.

He wasn't wrong. The narrow shopfront and the new home of Archer Fashion & Tailoring looked a little rough. Having moved in just days before, I technically had a sign above the door but it wasn't one I could be proud of. I just painted the name of the business on a piece of board and nailed it up, simply to have *something* to identify the business. When I had some time I would work on the sign above the door again.

The same front door that, at that very moment, was proving to be a major source of frustration.

"Well, if you come across any white paint I can use, you be sure to let me know, Mr. Culpepper." I frantically wiggled the key in the lock until it finally clicked free, the door opening with a comically loud squeak.

Closing the door behind me, I let out a long exhale. I put my new fabric away, flicked the lights on, and continued the work of setting things up. My new dress forms took pride of place in front of the windows where window shoppers could see the beautifully draped fabric I would use. My shiny new sewing machine sat in the back corner, handy to my large cutting table. I still needed a few things, odds and ends mostly, but it would do for now. It had to as I was quickly running out of funds and couldn't bear the thought of having to ask Gloria for more.

Since Cider Lane, named for a bootlegger who operated there in the late 1700s, was made up of tall and slender buildings of black and dark grey stone, not much light made its way into the one main window at the front or the small stained glass window above the door. The previous tenant of the space had thankfully made up for it by adding lots of overhead lighting.

I had hoped to find a retail space I could afford somewhere further west of Camden Town but the prices in places like St John's Wood, Primrose Hill, and Marylebone were far beyond my paltry budget.

I turned the sign in the front window, announcing that Archer Fashion & Tailoring was open for business and continued puttering around the shop, unpacking boxes of notions and supplies.

Mrs. Adams, a middle-aged woman I knew from Victoria's shop, let herself in, huffing and puffing and dragging four garment bags with her. She flung them on the front counter and let out an exaggerated sigh.

"I need you to let out these dresses, love," she announced between deep breaths. "I was going to replace them with new ones but I guess I won't be doing *that* now."

"Good morning, Mrs. Adams." I smiled sweetly at her. "Can I get you a cup of tea?"

Mrs. Adams inspected me a moment, frowned and then nodded reluctantly. "Thank you, dear."

I slid my sewing desk chair over to her so she could have a seat and went to the back of the shop to prepare her cup. "This clothing rationing scheme is one step too far if you ask me," she continued, speaking louder so I would hear her clearly. "First food, now clothing.

They didn't even give us a warning this time like they did with the food. That's just cruel!"

"They would have had people buying up all the clothes they could if they announced it beforehand," I said. "They wanted to make sure to keep things fair."

"Fair," she scoffed. "How is using sixteen coupons for an overcoat for my husband fair at all? How is *any* of this fair?"

As of the first of June, clothing was to be purchased with a combination of money *and* coupons, just like food. With a limit of sixty-six coupons per year, different articles of clothing were worth different numbers of coupons—a winter coat for a woman was worth fourteen coupons while a man's shirt was worth eight. With so much fabric going towards uniforms and other war essentials, a clothing ration was an unfortunate necessity that needed to be introduced to make sure the British population could stay clothed for however long the war lasted.

I had opened my shop just in time.

Since most of my work dealt with alterations, I wouldn't have to deal with coupons—unless, that is, someone had me create something for them from scratch.

I brought Mrs. Adams her tea. "All we can do is hope this war is over soon and clothing rationing won't have to last long. Now, tell me about the alterations we need for these dresses? Same as the last alterations?"

She sipped her tea and frowned. "Yes." She rolled her eyes. "I don't know how you managed to make the bust and hips bigger the last time."

I nodded. "How much more do you need me to add?"

"Three inches added to the bust." She shook her head and raised her gaze to the ceiling. "She's fourteen and looks like she's got two bloody footballs under her school uniform." Her lip curled. "When I was visiting her last weekend, she told me a few boys have started bothering her since she's…developing quickly."

Like many London teenagers and children, Mrs. Adams' daughter was living in the country until the government announced it was safe for them to be brought back. Like my aunt and uncle, some parents decided to bring their children back early, despite the risk of Blitz bombs. Mrs. Adams was following orders though and keeping her daughter at her mother's home, at least for now.

"Boys that age are the worst," I said, opening the garment bags to survey the dresses. "What about her school uniforms?"

"My mum said she'll alter those for her." She shook her head. "So, who knows how they'll end up. But nobody sews like you and Victoria can. Shame about her shop." Glancing around, she cocked an eyebrow. "But I guess it's not a total loss, eh?"

I shrugged. "Opportunities come in all forms."

At the end of my busy day I was about to flip the sign to closed and put the blackout curtains up when a familiar face appeared through the glass of the front window.

I whipped the door open. "Irene! I haven't seen you in ages."

Irene Haley, the prettiest girl on our street where we grew up in Deptford, smiled wide. "I saw your ad in the paper and had to come see it for meself." She glanced inside. "Oh, you were just closin' up. I'm so sorry. I tried to get here earlier—"

"Oh, hush," I said. "Come in, come in."

I was impressed she spotted my ad in the newspaper at all. It was only a tiny box of text in the bottom corner of the page as it was all I could afford. I locked the door and flipped the sign once she was in so we wouldn't be disturbed.

"It's so good to see you," I said, letting myself take in every detail of her cherubic face and slender frame.

"It's been a few years, hasn't it?" I offered her the chair I kept at the sewing machine while I hopped up on the counter I used as a cutting table. "Tell me everything. How is your mum? And the little ones? You've got three if I remember right."

"Four now." Irene's eyes were somehow warm and sad at the same time. "And Mum's moved in with us now since her health isn't what it used to be."

Her eyelids looked heavy and her shoulders were slack. Her face wasn't made up and she kept her cloche hat on, making me wonder right away if she'd had time to do her silky cinnamon brown tresses that morning—probably not, I assumed.

The war affected us all in a myriad of ways. Some of us simply hid it more effectively behind cosmetics and curls.

"I'm sorry to hear that, love," I said.

It was strange to think of her mother in poor health. I practically lived at Irene's growing up and her mum seemed capable of taking care of everyone and everything on about an hour of sleep.

"How is Eddie?"

Irene's brother Eddie was the third Musketeer in our little gang. The three of us got up to all kinds of mischief as children. Eddie, unfortunately, continued getting into mischief in his adolescent years and bounced in and out of jail.

"He's down at the docks. Staying out of trouble these days," she said. "I'm just grateful he's not away somewhere with a gun or grenades or any of that."

"Glad to hear it." I crossed my ankles. "And how about the little ones?"

Irene pressed her lips firm as her eyes went somber. "I haven't seen my babies in over two years. I'm afraid they won't remember me when they come back to London. They won't remember their own mum."

"I'm sure that's not true. Of course they'll remember you."

"They might not," she croaked. "One of my neighbors just brought her daughters back and they cried and cried at the train platform because they wanted to go back to the country. And now I'm…"

Her hand went protectively to her belly.

My brows went up. "Number five?"

She nodded slowly. "I'm happy. I am, really. Things are just hard right now, you know. We had to move to a smaller place since our home was bombed. When I bring the children back, I don't know how we'll all fit." She released a feeble chuckle, her voice crinkling at the edges.

"Oh, Irene. I'm so sorry."

"At least Howie is home safe. Thank God for that. He was injured and they sent him back to England," she clarified and studied the floor. "He's angry all the time. He drinks. It's like he's a different man." She cleared her throat. "I take care of him and Mum so I can't work outside the home and I miss my babies so much."

Irene's dam of emotions had obviously been threatening to burst long before visiting me. I wondered if she had anyone sympathetic to talk to at all.

I hopped down from the table as she stood.

"I should go," she said between sniffs. "I shouldn't be telling you all this when we haven't seen one another in so long—"

Wrapping my arms around her shuddering body as the sobs shook her slender frame, I rubbed her back and held her. She was far too thin for a pregnant woman.

"It's okay," I whispered. "You cry as much as you need to."

I hated the English adage of taking everything with a stiff upper lip because showing weakness was letting the Nazis win. It was all bollocks.

After her tears finally ran out, she stepped back and wiped her face with the backs of her hands. "I guess it's good I can't afford makeup because it would be all over your shoulder now."

My gaze landed on a small pile of garments nearby, sparking an idea. "I know you said you can't work outside the home but would you have time to take in some mending? You're still good with a needle and thread I bet."

Irene sniffed again. "I'm not bad."

"Would you be able to handle my overflow work? With the new clothes rationing scheme, I'm getting orders for clothing alterations. I could send you some mending work and pay you for it. It probably wouldn't be a lot of money but—"

"I'll take it," she said. "I'll take whatever you've got."

I nodded. "Perfect. Can I buy you supper? Do you have time?"

"I should get back," she said. "Mum has likely killed Howie by now so I'll have to clean up the mess." A little laugh escaped her lips. She looked at me for a long moment. "God, I miss you."

I hugged her again and we walked to the bus stop, chatting about old times.

We parted ways as my bus went north and her bus went south.

four

JACK

———※———

"You can't possibly be done moving all your things," Mrs. Sampson said, raising an eyebrow at the relatively small stack of boxes at the foot of the stairs up to the garret.

I winced. "Well, you see, I *did* have a few more belongings but…"

Her eyes grew wide. "But you lost them in a raid. Oh my god, I completely forgot. I'm so sorry. I'm such a git. Forget I said anything." She threw her hands up in the air and fled downstairs, leaving before she said anything else uncouth.

Nora leaned in the doorway of her nearby bedroom. "Don't take it personally. She said the same thing to me when I moved in." She crossed her slender arms over her chest and eyed the boxes. "Got anything interesting in there?"

"Not really. Some clothes. A few books. More books than clothes, I'll be honest." I piled three boxes and lifted them and then promptly set them back down again. "Two. I should have gone with two."

Nora giggled and two dimples appeared in her cheeks. "Here, let me help."

She grabbed a box and climbed the steep stairs to the attic after me.

Once all boxes were upstairs, she took a seat on my twin bed, admiring the old beams above us.

The image of Nora asleep on my chest that night in the tube station flashed in my mind. I wondered if her hair still smelled of gardenias.

Her wavy strawberry blonde hair was styled into submission. However, the trek up and down the stairs had caused a stray curl to come unpinned, and I forced myself not to reach out and tuck it behind her ear.

It's what Clark Gable would have done. Unfortunately, I was no Clark Gable.

"It's nice up here. I hope it doesn't get too warm in the summer," she said, leaving the bed and drifting to the little window.

The bed was against one wall, directly under one of the two sloped ceilings. I'd already bumped my head twice and knew I would have to be careful waking up each morning. A modest desk and chair were under the window at the back, a small desk lamp added since it was quite dark up there, even at midday. I didn't have a wardrobe yet but figured the trunk at the end of the bed would suit me well enough. A few boxes of dusty holiday decorations, trinkets, and cobwebs were tucked into the corner by the stairs.

"It beats Francis' couch certainly," I said, hoping I wouldn't have any rodent visitors in my new home.

"I would imagine so." She clasped her hands together. "Well, I better leave you to it."

"Before you go, can I ask you something?"

My heart leapt in my chest as her eyes, nearly the color of amber, met mine.

"Yes?"

I swallowed and suddenly regretted opening my mouth. But it was too late to go back now.

"If we had found one another again under different circumstances and I asked you to dinner, would you have said yes?"

Nora's red lips, matching the color of her floral frock, spread into a coy smile. "Perhaps."

"I'll take that as a yes."

"I guess we'll never know what could have been," she said, sauntering away.

"So, you're saying it's entirely off the table now?"

"That's what I'm saying," she said, starting down the stairs. "Alas."

Since I had stored a few things at my parents' house in St John's Wood, I took a bus there that afternoon. Only a short walk from the London Zoo, the street I grew up on was lined with leafy trees, perfectly manicured shrubs, and pristine wrought iron gates.

Only a building here and there showed signs of damage but this area of London—full of people who could actually afford to rebuild if they had to—managed to avoid the worst of the raids.

It was entirely unfair.

George, a member of the staff, let me in, his manner as stoic as ever.

"George, good fellow, how are you?"

He furrowed his brow. "You should speak with your mother, Mr. Parker. I believe she is in your father's office."

I rushed to the back of the house. The office door was open but I still gave a gentle knock as I was trained to do since childhood.

Mum looked over her shoulder at me from her place on the chaise, tear stains on her cheeks. My stepfather nodded in greeting from behind his inhumanly tidy mahogany desk, a recognizable piece of official letterhead in front of him. There was no mistaking it—it was from the British Army.

"What's happened? Is Archie—"

"He's been captured," Father said, his eyes glued to the letter.

I looked to my mother, her shoulders shaking and lips pressed firm.

Archie, my younger half brother, was serving in the army somewhere in northern Africa, although we weren't sure where. A natural athlete, smart and charismatic, Archie was good at everything and flourished during military training. If he could be captured by the enemy, then anyone could.

Father glared down at the letter like it had personally put his son in danger.

"Those useless bastards," he said, voice deepening. "His

commander probably sent him on some mission and didn't give him adequate backup and now look what's happened."

Mum released an unsteady breath. "Knowing him, he went back to save an injured friend and then he…he…" She put her hand over her quivering mouth.

Taking off his round spectacles and tossing them roughly onto the desk, Father sat back in his chair and closed his eyes, a deep crease forming between his brows. His chest heaving and his jaw clenched, my father darted right passed grief and bolted straight for fury.

I knew there was no point in offering my stepfather any comforting words. The only person he would accept those sentiments from were my mother and she was in no state for that.

Father straightened, slid his spectacles back on, gestured to the door, and picked up his phone. "I have to make some calls."

Quickly wiping her eyes, Mum took my arm and I closed the door behind us. Father's textile factories were converted to manufacturing uniforms for the military so he had contacts at the War Office. He wasn't the type to call in favors, but I knew he would when it came to his son.

I took Mum to her sitting room and one of the staff—a new girl, I didn't know her name—brought us some tea. Mum reached for the teapot with shaking hands so I quickly intercepted and poured for her, making sure to only fill it halfway.

"Thank you, dear," she said, carefully patting her cheeks with a napkin. "I knew this day could come. I thought maybe we would get lucky and he would stay safe."

"Maybe they can trade prisoners and get him back. Captured isn't, well, it's not the worst possible news."

I dared not say the dreaded D word.

"Archie was so excited to go to war. If he wasn't to take over the business, he would be an excellent general or captain or whatever," Mum said. "He's a natural leader. People love him."

I did not need to be reminded.

Prepared from birth, Archie seemed happy to take on the responsibility of the family business. If his enthusiasm for textile manufacturing was put on, I certainly couldn't tell.

Although he and I both went to Harrow as boys, I was allowed to flourish in academia while Archie took his place at Father's side as soon as he deemed Archie old enough.

Mum looked up at me. "If something were to happen to him—"

"Archie will be fine—"

"*If* something were to happen to him," she started again, closing her green eyes, "you'd have to take his place."

Piecing together what she meant, I blinked at her a moment. "The factories?"

I was the older brother but because I was the stepson and not the "real" son, Father had believed me unworthy of inheriting the factories, a responsibility I was happy to avoid.

But if the worst should happen and Archie didn't come home…

My guts turned. I hadn't even considered that.

I instantly recoiled at my own selfishness. He was serving his country in the desert, probably in some horrible POW camp, and I was scared I would have to be a businessman and leave my dusty archives and research behind at Cambridge for good.

"He'll come home," I said firmly. "Don't worry. Archie would never let us down."

five

Nora

———❖———

"How's the shop?" Jack carefully spread a tiny blob of margarine on his toast at breakfast, trying his best to make the ration go further.

Seeing him every morning and then almost every evening on a daily basis was leading me to distraction. There was nothing between us, of course, but seeing him so often just…threw me off, I suppose.

"It's good," I said, leaving out the bit about my stream of customers gradually slowing down. "How's school?"

"Good."

"Tell me about that student who was causing you trouble again," I said with a mischievous smirk. "Martin something? Sounds like a proper rascal."

"Oh, yes. You must be speaking of Marvin," Jack said, playing along. "Such a firebrand."

Marvin laughed across the table. "Hey, I am not!"

Jack put his hand over his mouth. "Goodness, I completely forgot. Oh, that's awkward. I mean, uh, it's a different Marvin, not you."

I laughed and bit my lip as Jack winked at Marvin.

"Just because you live in the same house that doesn't mean I want you to go easy on my boy," Uncle Harry said, finishing off his tea and sliding his chair out from the table.

"But you needn't be tougher on him either," Gloria added as Harry went upstairs to finish getting ready for the day.

"He treats me like he treats everyone else," Marvin added, toast crumbs collecting on his chin.

"And is he one of your nicer teachers or is a mean one?" I glanced at Jack as I propped my elbow up on the table and rested my cheek in my palm.

"He's one of the nicer ones. He doesn't yell like some of the other teachers," Marvin glanced at Jack. "Well, most of the time."

Gloria stood and kissed the top of Marvin's head. "You better go brush your teeth, dear, and don't forget to comb your hair." She began collecting the cups and plates and disappeared into the kitchen.

As Marvin scurried from the table, I raised an eyebrow at Jack. "Do you scream at those poor children?"

"Of course I don't," he said. "Sometimes you need to, well, raise your voice a little to get their attention."

I shook my head and sighed. "I never took you for a cruel schoolmaster, Mr. Parker."

"I'm Mr. Parker now, am I? Why does it sound so mocking when you say it?" His eyes narrowed slightly and his lip curled into a wicked grin.

"Because I'm mocking you."

The warmth in his eyes and the way they quickly grazed my neck made me blush.

"So, do you think any girls in the class have a crush on you?" I sat back in my chair. "I believe *I* fancied a teacher when I was that age."

Without missing a beat, Jack replied, "Do you fancy a teacher now?"

I studied his face for any hint of sincerity before picking up my tea again. I would not be thrown by his directness.

"No," I said, taking a moment to sip my tea. "I find them rather vain."

Jack laughed. "Vain?"

"Exactly." I smiled wide at him. "And smug."

He placed both hands over his chest. "I am positively wounded."

I sipped my tea again. "You'll live."

When I arrived at the shop that morning, Irene was already there waiting for me.

"Is everything alright?" I jogged down the pavement to reach her.

She nodded frantically and looked over her shoulder. "Yes, well, mostly. I just needed to come see you about something. I hope that's alright."

"Of course." I scrambled for my keys in my bag and let us in, keeping the sign showing 'Closed' so we could have privacy.

She wrapped her arms around herself, avoiding meeting my eye line, and anxiously picked at a loose thread on her well-worn skirt.

"Irene? Are you sure everything is alright?"

Irene shook her head. "I wish I didn't have to do this but you have to know how desperate I am."

"Are…are you robbing me?"

She chuckled. "No." She let out an unsteady breath, unlatched her purse, and pulled a cardboard sleeve out. She carefully placed it on the cutting table and stared at it like it might reach out and bite her.

It was a pair of silk stockings. I didn't recognize the hot pink packaging but they looked very high quality. Silk stockings were nearly impossible to come by since all newly manufactured silk went to the making of parachutes for the troops. Any available stockings were priced so high they were out of range for most people, but most sold out straight away no matter the cost. Some women had even begun staining their legs brown with tea bags or washable paint and drawing a "seam" up the back of their leg to make it look like they were wearing stockings. A few of the more daring women went without stockings entirely. I considered myself a modern woman but I had yet to go that far. Maybe in time I'd have to.

I waited for Irene to explain, but she just chewed on the skin around her thumbnail, the pace of her breathing steadily increasing.

Picking up the sleeve I inspected the package closely. "Where did you get these?"

"I have about fifty pairs," she exclaimed, disregarding my question.

"Fifty pairs of silk stockings?" I repeated, staring at her. "Where did you…" I closed my eyes. "He didn't. Tell me he didn't."

"Eddie only wanted to help me," she blurted, her words spilling out fast. "He knows I want to bring the children home and he knows I can't afford to keep all of us fed. So he grabbed a few pairs of stockings when unloading a cargo ship."

A few? Since when is fifty pairs of stockings a "few"?

Dropping the package, I stepped away from the table. My mind raced.

I wanted to ask if she knew how much trouble Eddie could get into. I wanted to ask if she knew how much trouble *she* could get into if someone found out she had taken them off his hands. I wanted to ask her how her husband and mother would take care of themselves while Irene was in prison. I wanted to ask how she could afford to care for her children if she was fined instead of imprisoned.

I knew asking was pointless. None of that mattered anyway, not really. The deed was done.

"Why did you bring this here? What do you want me to do with it?" I crossed my arms over my chest.

Someone walked by the front store window and I snatched the package out of view, shoving it back into her bag.

"I…" Irene blinked her big round eyes, and for a moment I thought she might cry. "I thought you might be able to sell them to your wealthy clients."

My eyebrows shot up. "Are you mad?"

Her gaze fell to the floor. "You're right. I'm sorry. I shouldn't have asked. I just didn't know…" After a moment she looked up at me again and set her shoulders back. Her face was stern, all previous fear hidden behind glassy eyes. "I'm doing what I have to do, and if you care about me at all you will help me do this."

"You can't just sell them yourself?"

"Who the bloody hell would I sell them to, the butcher's wife?" Irene placed her hands on the table between us. "Please Nora. I don't have anyone else I can ask. We'll split the takings fifty-fifty. I don't want Eddie to have risked everything for me for nothing."

"Eddie doesn't want a cut?"

"No, God bless 'im."

He was a scheming fool but his love for his sister was unparalleled.

I placed my hands on my hips and paced, weighing the pros and cons.

"Are you sure you want to bring your children home? Just because there hasn't been a raid in a few weeks doesn't mean they're done for good. What if—"

"Lots of people have brought their wee ones home already," she explained, sounding rehearsed. "Our new place isn't as close to the river so it should be okay. If the raids start again I'll send them away again, I swear. But as of right now, I can't even afford to go north to visit them."

"But you're pregnant. You shouldn't even be in London either."

She tilted her head at me.

"But you can't leave. Right," I said. Pacing a bit more, I groaned loudly. "Fine. I'll do it."

Irene threw her arms around me. "You have no idea how much this means to me."

"But I'm not taking a cut."

"What? No, you—"

"I mean it," I snapped. "Don't argue with me or I'll change my mind."

Her eyes welled with tears again. "You are an angel, you know that?" She rested her head on my shoulder and squeezed me. "Thank you."

She handed me the single pair of stockings from her bag and promised Eddie would deliver the full case late the following day. I just nodded and gave a little wave as she left to catch her bus home.

As soon as the door closed behind her, I closed my eyes and released a long breath. I gently lowered my forehead to the counter and bounced it against the smooth wood several times, hoping one of the bumps to the head would eventually knock some sense into me.

six

JACK

———◆———

"I know it sounds terribly stupid but sometimes I think I'd rather be shooting Nazis in some African desert than teaching twelve-year-olds about history."

Francis frowned at me from across our usual table at our go-to pub, The Ox and Crane. "You're right. That *does* sound terribly stupid."

The barmaid slid our beers onto the table, a tiny bit of foam spilling out over the rims.

"I'm a fool. I know," I said, reaching for my pint. "I am very aware of it."

Francis glanced at the barmaid and then looked back at me. "You're so wrapped up in your whole self-pitying academic act that you didn't catch that gorgeous bird making eyes at you."

"Oh? I didn't notice."

Francis rolled his eyes before studying my face for a moment. "Did something happen?"

"Hmm?"

"You're off with the fairies, mate."

"Ah. Sorry," I mumbled. "We got some news about my brother

recently." I lowered my voice and checked over my shoulder for…I don't know, Nazi spies or some such nonsense. Even from our booth I could see one of the government's "Loose Lips Might Sink Ships" posters on the wall. "He's been captured by the Italians."

Francis growled an offensive slur. "I'm sorry. Your mum must be off her hinges with worry."

I nodded. "She's trying hard to put on a brave, positive face but I think that's for my stepfather's benefit more than anything else."

In fact, I was almost certain that was the case. Showing emotion was weakness and weakness meant losing the war, even if only on the morale front. It was all hogwash, of course.

"That's terrible." Francis shook his head. "I've got two brothers in north Africa. Sounds like a bloody nightmare."

"Captured isn't killed," I said, mostly to remind myself that hope remained.

"Cheers to that," Francis said, lifting his glass.

We clinked glasses and drank.

After a moment of companionable silence, Francis sat back on his side of the booth. "How's the new living situation?"

I chuckled lightly, rubbing the back of my neck. "Well, uh, mostly good. It's a lovely house, it's close to school, I have my own space, and Mrs. Sampson is a great cook."

"Sounds ideal."

"There *is* one slight hitch. Do you remember Nora? Cal's girl's friend? She came to the pub and I ended up offering to walk her home but we got lost in the dark and ended up sleeping at Blackfriars station together?"

He shrugged. "No?"

"Well, I told you about her. I'm sure I did," I scoffed. "Well, she lives there too. Mrs. Sampson is her aunt."

Francis let out a loud bark of laughter. "You finally found her again and you can't do anything about it. Incredible."

"See, you *do* remember."

"Vaguely."

"But yes, that's the problem. I see her at breakfast and I see her in the evening and I can't bloody ask her on a proper date because we live together."

"So find somewhere else to live."

"Well. Aren't you the romantic?" I snickered. "I can't afford to rent anywhere else close to Highgate. I looked already."

"Don't your parents live up that way?"

"I'm not moving back in with my parents. I would go mad."

"Sounds like you're likely going to go mad living with this girl anyway."

I considered this. "You make a good point."

"But before you do anything foolish like find a flat or move back in with Mum and Dad, you should probably know if she'd say yes or no," he suggested. "Or…"

"Or?"

"*Or* the two of you have some fun in secret while living in the same house until you make a mess of it and she breaks it off and *then* you find another place to live because you can't stand how uncomfortable it is to eat breakfast across the table from a fine woman who hates your guts."

"Why do I get the feeling you've already done this?"

"I am a man of the world."

"You've never been out of England."

He raised his pint in salute.

"I have a family thing coming up in a few weeks," I said with a dismissing wave. "I know they'll want me to bring someone as a date and if I don't bring Nora, Mum will set me up with this daughter of a friend." I groaned. "She might not be ready for my family though. Spending time with them would scare anyone off."

Francis wrinkled his nose and recoiled slightly. "Christ, you're not a member of the royal family or something, are you?"

"No," I laughed. "They're just…they're a bit much."

"Well, if she likes you at all, perhaps 'a bit much' is her style."

I shot him a look.

"Speaking of the fairer sex," I said, eager to change the subject, "what happened with that woman who was walking around nearly naked at your flat?"

"I like her quite a bit."

My eyes widened. "I don't believe it. Have you finally met someone you might want to marry?"

Francis snorted with laughter. "I don't think her husband would like that very much."

With hops and barley boosting my confidence I returned home to Highgate later that evening. My face felt a little warm as I let myself into the house, struggling to get the key to cooperate for a moment.

Quiet but peppy jazz music played on the wireless at the far end of the living room. Nora smiled sweetly up at me from the couch and set her knitting down on her lap—I felt that smile all the way down to my toes. With her legs tucked under her, her feet poked out to the side and the hem of her navy blue and white plaid dress had slid up above her knees.

"Good evening, stranger," she said. "Out on a school night?" She pursed her lips and arched an eyebrow.

Fearing nervousness if I sat beside her, I took a seat in the armchair across from her and forced myself not to gawk at her lovely legs. "I was supporting a small business. Don't you know there's a war on? *I am a hero.*"

Her whole face lit up as she laughed. "Oh, well, in that case, carry on."

I pointed to the needles and yarn. "What are you up to?"

"Baking a cake." She picked up the needles again and they clicked as she grinned at me.

"I meant 'what are you knitting?'"

"Socks for the soldiers."

I was transfixed as her fingers worked the needles so quickly, loops forming seamlessly while she seemed to barely look at what she was doing.

"How do you *do* that?"

"A lot of practice," she said. "My mum taught me when I was five or six. It was cheaper to make things like socks and mittens and jumpers than buy them new. A few years later I learned to sew."

"And the rest is history."

"Aye."

"Where's your mum and dad? Are they in London?"

"No." Nora's face stiffened. "My father died when I was seven and I believe my mother is in Swindon."

She isn't certain where her mother is?

"Oh. I'm sorry," I said. "My father died when I was three."

I was used to getting looks of pity when I shared that personal fact about myself, but Nora looked at me with more curiosity than sympathy.

She paused her knitting. "I thought you said your father owned a textile factory."

"That's my stepfather. I call him my father but he and Mum married when I was six."

The song on the wireless changed from a jumpy jazz tune to the gentle melody of "Dream a Little Dream of Me." I flashed a smile at Nora and she arched an eyebrow again. She was very good at that.

I stood, stuck my hands in my pockets, and shimmied over to the couch, bouncing my shoulders along with the tune. Nora bit her lip, trying not to laugh at my ridiculous attempt to be charming.

"I've had enough beer tonight to ask you to dance with me."

"Right here in the living room?"

I offered her my hand. She considered for a moment, her gaze bouncing between my hand and my eyes. Finally she set her knitting aside and slid her soft, smooth hand into mine.

She maintained eye contact for a moment as she placed her other hand on my shoulder. Her gaze never faltered as my palm slid down to her lower back, my mind committing to memory every ripple of fabric between us and every coil of sunset-colored hair resting around her neck.

I wondered if Nora ever felt uncertain or insecure about anything. I had never met another woman who was so self-assured and so quick. I found it immensely attractive.

Nora finally set her gaze on our entwined fingers and adjusted her hand on my shoulder, subtly shrinking the space between us. My pulse quickened. She was close enough for me to whisper in her ear. Just a few words. That's all it would take. I felt the words forming on my tongue.

This was the moment, handed to me on a silver platter. This was it.

"How was your day?"

Not those *words, you idiot.*

Nora looked up at me again, puzzled. "What?"

"I just asked…how your day was."

"It was grand." She sounded slightly puzzled by the question. "And yours?"

"Uh, it was, uh, it was good."

An awkward silence wedged itself between us until Nora spoke up.

"Your students must be looking forward to the summer holidays coming up."

"Yes, certainly," I said. *God, you smell so good.* "Exams first though."

"Right."

I spent the rest of the song clenching my jaw and feeling disgusted with myself. I never had trouble talking to women before.

As the song ended, Nora slowly slid herself away from me. She switched off the side lamp by the couch and picked up her knitting, sharing a small smile with me.

"Good night, Jack."

"Good night." I gave a single nod and switched off the wireless.

A few minutes later I stretched out on my bed and stared at the beams above me, wondering what I had just done and why I couldn't have simply asked her to the event like I planned. Why? Why couldn't I have just said the right words?

She's probably sitting on her bed right now, asking herself what the bloody hell is wrong with that weird man?

I groaned and rolled over in bed. If I had ruined our playful, lovely, flirtatious back-and-forth with my sudden social ineptitude, I would be furious with myself.

seven

Nora

—⟡—

When one works alone for hours, deeply focused on a task, it can sometimes feel almost magical. Sewing, for me, was like breathing. Breath in, needle up through fabric, breath out, needle down through fabric. Stitch, snip, stitch, snip.

However, when one is working on a task they've done thousands of times before, their mind tends to wander to places it shouldn't go.

Like back to the living room the evening before. Jack's eyes gazing into mine like he could read my thoughts. The two of us swaying smoothly to the music from the wireless. His hand skimming over my dress as he moved it to the small of my back.

Thinking of it made heat rise in my neck and caused my cheeks to flush. It had been a long time since I'd felt so…vulnerable around a man—like there was a chance he could ask something outrageous of me and I would actually go along with it, just because his smile was dazzling. Just because I felt warm when he looked at me. Just because my heart raced when we touched.

I hated that feeling. It wasn't kind to me in the past.

What would have happened if I hadn't fled from him last night?

The front door of the shop clicked open and I nearly jumped out of my skin. I'd been staring into the middle distance at my sewing machine for who knows how long. Thank goodness I wasn't ironing while my mind wandered—I could have burned the place down.

"Mrs. Garnier, good morning! You're here for your coat, yes?" I hopped up from my machine and rifled through the clothing rack near the front counter. "I think you'll be quite happy with how it turned out."

The week before Mrs. Garnier, a woman of perhaps forty-five, brought me her lovely dark tan winter coat with a worn out interior lining and a like-new man's winter coat with a pristine satin houndstooth print lining. I wasn't even sure the man's coat had even been worn. She requested I take the lining from the man's coat and put it in her winter coat. Otherwise she would have to spend fourteen coupons on a new coat.

"We bought it shortly before the war," Mrs. Garnier explained. "If only I'd known, I mightn't have bothered buying the coat for him."

"I'm so sorry for your loss," I said, solemnly checking the lining while we spoke.

"Pardon me?"

"Oh, I assumed he…"

She burst out laughing. "Oh, goodness, no, darling," she said, rolling her eyes. "It's not as macabre as all that. We got a divorce. He's married to his secretary now and I married an artist." She leaned in, despite there being nobody else in the shop besides us. "He's French and twelve years younger than me."

"Bravo, good for you," I said, genuinely impressed.

I wondered if Mrs. Garnier and her former spouse would have stayed married if the war hadn't come along and opened their eyes to their unhappy situation.

Setting the new and improved coat on the counter for her, I spread out the lapels so she could check my handiwork.

"It looks perfect. Wonderful work," she said, peeking into the sleeve. "I don't think anyone could even tell it wasn't a brand new coat."

"Excellent. I'm so glad you're pleased." I placed the folded lining-free coat up on the counter beside it. "I assume you want this back. Perhaps Mr. Garnier might like it? With a new lining put in it before winter, of course."

She sighed. "I suppose I should take it home. I might regret it later if I don't."

"Probably a wise plan."

I was about to tally her total when the small wooden crate—hidden under an orange tea towel below the front counter—caught my eye, and I stopped myself. Mrs. Garnier seemed modern and composed, unruffled by the stigma of both a divorce *and* marrying a considerably younger chap.

Clearing my throat, I lowered my eyes. "Mrs. Garnier, how are you doing for…" I winced and tried again. "Would you be interested in…"

She hard blinked at me. "Are you having some kind of episode?"

I let out a breath and blurted, "As you know, I am a young woman trying to run a new business on my own and I have a, um, clothing accessory in my possession that is very hard to find. I am selling them off-ration." I bit my lip and watched her reaction.

Mrs. Garnier tilted her head like a curious dog but looked generally unmoved by my confession. "What kind of clothing accessory exactly?"

"Silk stockings," I whispered. "Quite nice ones."

"Can I see them?"

Swiftly moving around the counter, I checked the front window and locked the door.

She smirked. "This is all very cloak and dagger. I feel like a spy."

I slid one of the sleeves onto the counter for her to inspect.

She barely glanced at it. "Can I buy four pairs?"

After she paid a reasonable price for the coat alterations and a hefty sum for the stockings I slid them all into paper bags, making sure to wrap the stockings in the coats to hide them.

"If you have friends who you trust to be discreet, please let them know I have stockings to sell," I said with a stern nod.

Mrs. Garnier gave a single nod back. "Understood."

The following day, a pretty woman with perfect chin-length blonde curls hesitantly stepped into the shop.

"Good morning," I said, finishing off a seam and tying the ends off. "How can I help you?"

The woman, a tiny thing in her early twenties or so, glanced around the shop and gripped the strap of her bag with gloved hands. She didn't have any garments with her.

"Good morning," she said in an accent one might describe as a bit snooty. "What a lovely little shop this is."

I smiled at her as she took a closer look at a nearby dress form where one of my works in progress waited for me to get back to it.

The young woman wore a very chic and flawlessly tailored two-piece ensemble—almost certainly couture. With its matching fascinator, square shoulders, and black buttons that went down the front and carried on down the knee-length skirt, the outfit perfectly suited the current trend of military-influenced fashion for women.

She was obviously wealthy but hadn't brought in a garment to alter. There was only one other thing she could be in my "lovely little shop" for. But I certainly wasn't going to bring it up first.

"This is quite fetching," she said, her eyes wide in genuine surprise, delicately lifting up the pear green fabric. "Is this for sale?"

"No, sorry, that's something I'm working on for a client," I explained, sliding in behind the front counter. "She brought in that gorgeous green dress and an older beaded blouse that were close to the same color. I made some adjustments to the dress and then took fabric from the blouse to change up the bodice."

"It's divine," she said, gazing at it wistfully.

"I'm pleased you like it," I said. "I mostly do alterations but sometimes I get to have some fun and do projects where I make something entirely new. That's what I want to do eventually—design clothes, I mean."

She finally looked back at me and approached the counter. "Forgive me. I'm actually not here for your sewing skills."

"Oh?"

"No. Not as such." She set her bag on the counter and gripped her hands together in front of herself. "My friend, Mrs. Garnier, said you might have some items for sale." She checked over both shoulders and raised her eyebrow meaningfully. "And off-ration?"

I moved to lock the door. The young woman swallowed hard as I returned to my post behind the counter.

"Stockings," she finally whispered. "I can't find any place that has any in, and I only have three pairs left. It's absolutely catastrophic."

I almost laughed. There were women walking around London wearing the same rough-looking stockings daily. To have three pairs of stockings was to have treasure in your possession.

Just like I did with Mrs. Garnier, I pulled a pair of stockings from the crate and slid them onto the counter so this lady could have a look. And, also like Mrs. Garnier, she barely took any time to look at them before asking how many she could buy.

I accepted her money and tucked it into an envelope inside the crate as the blonde woman secreted her new stockings safely into her bag. I'd give the money to Irene the next time I saw her.

Before she left, the woman stopped at the dress form again and ran a finger over the silky material, considering.

She looked at me over her shoulder, her green eyes sparkling.

"I want something new. Something different that nobody else will have," she announced. "I have no idea what garments I would bring down here for you to make something though." She turned to face me again. "If I paid for your time, could you come to my home in St John's Wood on Monday and look through my dressing room with me? I think it would be much easier if you were there so you could just tell me which of my old dresses you could use. That way you can see what my usual style is and you can see for yourself if a dress could be adapted."

I blinked at her. "Monday?"

She nodded, all confidence. "If possible. I have an event coming up in a few weeks so I would rather not wait. I don't need a quote. You can bill my father when we're finished."

I tried not to answer too quickly. "Yes, of course. We can certainly do that." I grabbed a pen and a piece of paper from under the counter.

"I'll just get your information and when you'd like me to be there."

"Topping." She jotted her name, address, and a time with elegant, flourish-heavy handwriting. "I will see you then. Shall I send a car to come round to pick you up?"

Staring at her for a moment, I realized she must live in an entirely different world than the rest of us. Were the upper classes secretly allowed to use petrol as much as they wanted?

"No, no. That's quite alright. Thank you for the kind offer though."

"Well, if you're sure. Cheerio."

I glanced at the name on the paper and gave a little wave as she sauntered past the front window.

Elsie Foster-Quinn, I am going to make so much money from you.

eight

JACK

"Jack? Are you up there?"

I bolted upright when I heard Nora calling me from the bottom of the stairs. Since it was Saturday afternoon I was working at my desk in my bedroom, trying to decide on questions for a test I had to give my pupils the following week. I was behind—I should have had it prepared the week before but my ability to focus was sliced in half since Archie went missing.

And, yes, I had to admit, since moving into the same house as Nora.

The speed at which I threw myself from my desk and down the stairs was, well, genuinely shameful.

I leaned a shoulder against the doorframe, feigning nonchalance. "Yes?"

Nora tilted her head slightly. "I didn't know you wore glasses."

"Oh. Right. They're just for reading. I forgot I still had them on."

She considered my face for a moment before giving a nod of approval. "They suit you. They make you look extra academic."

"I'll take that as a compliment."

"You should," she said. "So, Gloria needs a favor and I don't *really* want to do it by myself." She made an awkward little pleading cringe-smile.

"Do you have a bit of time to spare?"

You have assignments to mark, a test to prepare, and a lesson plan to—

"Sure. What are we up to this afternoon?"

Nora beamed and I felt my cheeks flush.

"Gloria is owed a cut of pork from a friend in Hampstead," she began. "I guess this friend needed some pork for her son's favorite dish while he was home so Gloria gave hers up. Now this friend has some pork to give her back. Gloria is in bed with a headache at the moment so I offered—on behalf of both of us—"

"Naturally."

"—to go and get it for her." She folded her hands behind her back. "I thought we could bike there since it's such a nice day out."

She's making an effort to spend time with me. I forced myself not to grin like an idiot.

I borrowed Mr. Sampson's bicycle while Nora rode Mrs. Sampson's. Stored in the garden shed, both bikes were dusty and stiff with disuse but functional enough for an afternoon ride. Nora's bike came with a basket in front so we could transport the meat home.

It was a gorgeous June afternoon. Highgate, with its views of central London, was at its peak. The area's abundance of mature trees were thick and bright with green foliage while front gardens and window boxes shared jolly splashes of pink, yellow, and blue.

"Do you know how to get there?" I asked as I began to pedal a little faster to keep up with her, following her down one street and then another.

"I think so," she called over her shoulder, several curls breaking free and whipping in the wind.

Once she slowed down slightly, we rode side by side.

"How's school?"

"Good. Although with the nicer weather, the kids are pining for the outdoors more often."

"So why not teach them outside?"

I frowned and put on a pompous, stuffy voice. "Highgate Grammar School is known for its exceptional standards of student achievement. No need to go messing about with new, radical methods of educating the pupils."

She laughed. "I see." Glancing at me, she said, "Do you miss your job at Cambridge?"

I let out a small groan. "Very much. But if this is where I'm most of use to the war effort, then I'll stay a teacher. I suppose I should feel grateful I'm not getting shot at."

"If you find me a gun, I could take a couple shots at you if you're that desperate."

"Why do I get the impression you're only half joking?"

She bared her teeth in a wide smile.

Eventually, Nora spoke up again. "You're not grateful to be serving somewhere safe?"

I followed her down another street. "I am grateful. I am. Sometimes I fear I'm not doing enough—for the war effort *or* as a teacher."

She looked back at me.

"I'm a rubbish teacher," I clarified.

"I'm sure that's not true," Nora said. "Marvin adores you. I don't think he would like you so much if you were actually rubbish."

"He's a good kid," I said. "Quite clever too. I'm surprised your aunt and uncle didn't send him to a public school."

"Gloria tried to get Uncle Harry to agree to send Marvin to Eton but Harry wasn't having it. He doesn't think the tuition cost would be worth it," she explained, stopping to take a breath. "I suppose *you're* an old Etonian."

"Old Harrovian," I corrected.

"Oh, sorry," Nora said, rolling her eyes. "And here I thought you were posh."

"Yes, yes, I know," I said. "Fancy boy went to a fancy school so he must be a snobbish prig—"

"I never said that."

I narrowed my eyes at her in mock annoyance and she began to pedal again.

"How are things at the shop?"

Hesitancy flashed across her face before she quickly wiped it away, replacing it with her usual placid smirk. "Good. I have a new client

I'm seeing on Monday. She wants me to make her something unique."

"Unique?" I repeated. "What, like something strange looking?"

"Something nobody else will have," she clarified. "Modern."

"Do you have any ideas?"

"Not yet," she said before tilting her chin up defiantly. "Inspiration cannot be chased. It must be found." She glanced back at me and picked up speed again.

"Wait, what does that even mean?" I called after her, pushing harder on the pedals.

After we found the house and got the pork wrapped in brown paper, we set off back for Highgate. When we arrived at Hampstead Heath, we took a moment to walk our bicycles between a few of the park's many ponds and to Parliament Hill, arguably the best spot in the city for views of central London.

Tragically, not even the heath remained untouched by the war. The green was pockmarked with disturbed soil where bombs had struck. Army cadets ran in tight formation through the paths and in between vegetable patches.

We mounted our bikes again. I pedalled in front of Nora, showing off. As I watched her over my shoulder, she flicked a curl away from her face and smiled wide at me. That smile would ruin me and I wouldn't even mind.

Nora's eyes suddenly widened. "Jack, watch out!"

I whipped my head just in time to see my bike heading directly for a woman and a gaggle of small children and I swerved to avoid them. My bike screeched with the sudden movement and I hurdled into what was directly to the right of the woman and gaggle of children—a pond.

The cool water sank deep into my clothes and made them heavy as I kicked and flailed my arms. As my head broke the surface, I spit out a mouthful of pond water.

"Bollocks," I shouted.

The woman I'd swerved to avoid glared and shooed the children away from me and my filthy words. Nora parked her bike and pulled my bicycle out of the water along the pond's edge. I didn't know how I was flung so far from my bike. I swam to the pond's edge and took

Nora's hand so she could drag me out.

Dripping wet, I scowled at my watery nemesis. Hearing a quiet snort from next to me, I looked at Nora, her lips clamped tight. I sighed at her as her mouth contorted, fighting back giggles.

"You think this is funny?"

That did it. She erupted with laughter, one hand on her stomach and half bent over.

"I can't believe that just happened," she sputtered, wiping the tears from her cheeks.

I grabbed her arm. "That's it. You're going in, too."

She squealed and yanked her arm away and I chased her around the side of the pond, her high-pitched shrieks and cackles alarming the nearby park patrons. She dashed into a cluster of trees and I went in after her.

"Bloody thing," I heard her say from behind a tree.

A rather impolite oak had reached out a gnarly branch and grabbed ahold of Nora's yellow plaid skirt, leaving a small rip in the fabric.

Winded, she cursed and let out a chuckle. "Stupid tree."

"I know someone who can fix that for you," I said.

"Oh? What's she like?" Her smile turned coy, her eyes darkening.

I stepped closer and she rested her back against the oak's trunk. The pounding of my heart sped up as I considered my reply.

"Extraordinary," I said, taking another step towards her.

Nora put her palms on my chest and said in a breathy voice, "You're soaking wet."

I lifted one of her hands from my damp shirt and kissed the top of it. Her soft skin smelled like mint. Nora's chest heaved and she glanced from my eyes to my mouth and back again. Her pink lips parted ever so slightly and she lightly tugged on my shirt, willing me closer. I lowered my mouth to meet hers.

A quiet titter from the left of us caught our attention and I jerked my head back up. Catching sight of two kids watching us from behind a tree, I quickly put some distance between Nora and I. The children scurried away, leaving the moment ruined in their wake.

Nora put her hand over her flushed face and laughed. "We should probably get back."

I followed her out of the wood. "Can I catch them first and throw *them* in the pond?"

After a delicious meal of pork and sideways glances between Nora and myself, I took advantage of the gorgeous evening and took my stack of assignments out to the back garden, setting myself up on the bench. Even as I underlined spelling mistakes, squinted at illegible words, and added notes to the margins, I was far from focused.

Bees flitted among the flower beds and rose bushes lining the fence. Most of the generous garden was taken up by raised garden vegetable patches, all exquisitely maintained. I wondered how many flower gardens Mrs. Sampson sacrificed to make room for food she could grow herself as the government advised, and how many flower gardens were sacrificed all over Britain. Nestled at the back of the garden, buried half into the dirt and reinforced with soil on top and sandbags along the sides, was an Anderson shelter.

I thought back to the days of sleeping in my local tube station while bombs crashed and boomed overhead. Some central Londoners still made their nightly pilgrimage to the shelters and tube stations, mostly to claim their space in case there *was* a raid. A false alarm hadn't even sung out into the night sky since I'd moved to Highgate. Getting to sleep in a bed was a luxury I would never take for granted again.

"I thought you might like some tea, professor," Nora said from behind me, sliding a cup and saucer onto the wee table beside the bench.

"Oh, thank you. That was very thoughtful of you."

She nodded and turned to go back inside.

"Sit with me a moment," I said. "It's such a nice evening."

I moved my papers aside so she could join me.

Sliding my glasses off, I massaged the bridge of my nose. I kept meaning to take them to the oculist to get them adjusted since they pinched my nose but it kept slipping my mind.

Nora plucked the frames off my lap and slid them onto her own face. She looked around a bit and then lifted them off her nose and put them back again.

"I don't even notice a difference."

"They're for reading. Believe me, I notice."

She slid them down with her finger and looked at me over the tops of them, arching an eyebrow. "Are you sure you don't just wear them to make you look smarter?"

"Yes, that's definitely it." I snickered. "I probably hurt my eyes from reading too many old documents in poorly lit libraries over the years. You just wait. After years of focusing on sewing, you'll need glasses at some point too."

She returned the glasses and I put them on again, pretending to go back to work on my assignments.

Nora sat back on the bench, gazed out into the garden, and crossed her legs.

Her long, alluring legs.

I forced my eyes back down to the stack of assignments I'd barely touched and picked up my pen again.

"I had fun today," she said after a long pause. "I haven't laughed like that in a long time."

"I'm glad my misfortune could entertain you." I glanced at her and smiled so she'd know I was joking.

The door out to the back garden creaked as Gloria wandered out, a cup of tea in hand.

Nora looked over her shoulder at her aunt. "Is your head still feeling alright?"

"Yes, it's fine, dear," Mrs. Sampson said. "Marvin broke the zipper on a pair of trousers. Could you take a look at it for me?"

"Of course." She tossed me a mischievous look using only her eyes before disappearing inside.

Mrs. Sampson took her place on the bench, sitting in silence for a moment that seemed to stretch on for ages.

"The meal this evening was wonderful," I said, desperate to fill the awkward space between us.

"Thank you. It's one of my mother's recipes. I had to make some substitutions, of course." She took a sip of tea. "But I'm surprised you noticed how it tasted. You were a bit preoccupied."

I swallowed. "What do you mean?"

She finally looked directly at me. "Something is going on between you and my niece. I had my suspicions before but you both made it abundantly clear this evening."

"Oh. That." I winced. "I would never—"

"I'm a traditional type of person, Mr. Parker. You seem like a nice boy and a gentleman but I have to insist that nothing…improper happens between the two of you while you are both residing in my home. I obviously have no objection to the two of you courting but if those are the plans, one of you will need to find an alternative living arrangement. I'm sure you understand."

And by "one of you," she obviously meant me specifically. She'd never turn Nora out.

"I would never—"

"Have I made myself quite clear, Mr. Parker?" Her mouth was curved like a smile but her eyes were cold and all business.

I hesitated and then nodded. "Yes. I understand."

Her face warmed. "Excellent. I'm glad we're in agreement." She stood and went back to the house. "I'll leave you to your marking."

Finding another place to live nearby I could actually afford was going to be impossible. I would never ask Nora to find somewhere else to live.

I sighed and stared into the garden, suddenly feeling the fierce desire to rip out the perfectly pruned tomato plants.

nine

Nora

———❦———

Even though I didn't join the Sampsons for church on Sundays, I always made sure to rise early to breakfast with them. On that particular Sunday, however, I got up even earlier to put on makeup, curl my hair and put on a pretty tulip yellow frock. I felt a bit guilty as I applied my lipstick, knowing it was a precious commodity and there I was, wasting it on *breakfast*.

But I wanted to look pretty for Jack. I could admit that.

I waited for him to come to the bottom of the stairs so I could "accidentally" emerge from my bedroom at the same time and throw him a charming smile. Just as I heard the stairs creaking under his feet, Marvin appeared in the hall, his golden hair combed neat and his shirt and trousers freshly pressed.

"Are you coming to church with us?"

I gave an awkward chuckle as Jack reached the bottom of the stairs. "No."

"Then why are you dressed fancy?" Marvin tilted his head at me. "You usually just go back to bed after breakfast on Sunday."

Thank you so *much, cousin.*

Jack and I exchanged glances as my cheeks burned. "I-I-I have plans with a friend after breakfast."

He seemed satisfied with that answer and jogged down the stairs ahead of us.

I raised my eyes to Jack, looking through my mascaraed lashes. "Good morning."

His mouth was a tight straight line and he didn't look at me as he murmured, "Morning," and hurried downstairs.

I stared at the back of his head as he left me alone on the landing, wondering what I did wrong. Following him down, I wordlessly took my usual seat at the dining table as Gloria served breakfast.

"Clothes rationing only started a week ago," Harry said between bites, "and the criminals are at it already."

I snapped my eyes to his end of the table. "What do you mean?"

He poked his finger at a story about a gang selling stolen shoes without coupons. I swallowed and stuffed a bit of sausage into my mouth.

"It was bound to happen, I suppose," Gloria sighed, lifting her tea to her lips before glancing to me. "Think you could sew a winter coat for my boy? I don't think his coat from last year will fit him come December and I would rather not use more coupons if I don't have to. I think I have some old fabric you can use."

I nodded. "Sure."

"People will start forging clothing coupons soon," Harry added. "You just wait."

Jack was silent throughout this exchange, just eating and staring at his plate. I'd become so used to exchanging little smiles and glances with him during mealtimes.

Maybe he's not feeling well? Going by the empty space on his plate, his appetite seemed fine. If anything, I would say he ate faster than—

Jack slurped the final gulp of his tea and wiped his hands on his napkin, rising. "Apologies, got to dash."

My shoulders fell as he disappeared round the corner, the sound of the front door shutting following.

Gloria raised an eyebrow. "Where's he off to so early on a Sunday morning?"

I tried to hide my look of disappointment behind my teacup. "No idea."

The next morning, Elsie Foster-Quinn led me through her grand bedroom and passed her canopy bed fit for a princess. I stopped to check out something I hadn't expected to find in her bedroom—an impressive collection of novels by Jane Austen, the Brontë sisters, George Eliot, and Elizabeth Gaskell. She had multiple versions of several Austen and Brontë novels—maybe all, I wasn't sure, many in full sets with the matching binding.

Elsie noticed me admiring her books. "Do you like Austen?"

I winced, feeling a bit common, and shrugged. "I read *Sense and Sensibility* in school. I'm not much of a reader."

"You should give Jane another shot," she said. "She really was very clever."

All I remembered about *Sense and Sensibility* was the one sister swooning over that one bloke and then marrying someone else at the end. That didn't sound terribly clever to me.

We carried on into Elsie's dressing room and my eyes bulged. I hadn't expected a room three times the size of my bedroom.

Shelves and shoe racks lined the back wall while the two side walls were dedicated to over a hundred garments hanging on wooden coat hangers, all lined up together like crayons in a box. The front wall where I stood, gobsmacked, was home to a mirror that reached the ceiling and an elegant antique vanity. In the middle of all of it was a chaise.

I wondered if Elsie felt the need to buy more clothes to fill up the vast storage space or if she ever had to make room for new clothes. From what I could tell, none of the outfits were particularly outdated either. I'd never seen anything like it.

"This room used to be used for servant's quarters but it made a lot more sense to use it for my clothes," Elsie said.

"It's incredible," I admitted.

While I took the train to St John's Wood earlier that day, I'd decided I would be better off acting nonchalant about her wealth. Then I stepped inside Elsie's extravagant home and that idea went entirely out the window. Everything sparkled—the magnificent chandeliers, the spotless marble floors, and the perfectly polished railing on the grandiose, sweeping staircase from the foyer.

My humble beginnings involved sharing a bedroom with a sibling and skipping meals when pennies needed pinching. Setting foot into that house was like visiting another planet.

"To get a better sense of your current style, can you pull four or five of your favorite outfits?" I suggested. "Maybe begin with a dress or two?"

She crossed the floor and slid the outfits apart to access a deep blue floor length gown with long sleeves, a high neckline and a gold ring at the cinched waist. It was simple but elegant.

"I wore this a few months ago," she said. "It might be a bit too elegant for this event…"

She pulled another dress—this one was knee-length and made from a cheerful red-orange fabric with white floral embroidery along the hem and up near the voluminous shoulders. She held it out in front of herself at arm's length and studied it.

"What type of event is it?"

"It's a fundraiser." Elsie put the dress back on the rack and kept browsing. "We're raising money to help war widows who have lost their homes in the raids. We're hosting a formal dinner and then cocktails in the evening."

"Oh, that sounds like fun."

Elsie rolled her eyes. "Only if you enjoy the company of men too old to go to war."

I released a light laugh. "Do you have a beau overseas?"

"Nothing serious thankfully. The chap I was writing to—mostly out of pity more than anything else—he decided he'd rather shack up with a farmer's daughter in Scotland while he's stationed there. Can you imagine?" She rolled her eyes again and laughed, pulling another gown from the rack.

"Oh, what's that?" I rose from the chaise to inspect it closer.

Elsie pulled the long white sheath dress out. "This? Really? There's not much to it."

"Yet," I said. "There's not much to it *yet*. Unless you don't want me altering this one."

"Have at it," she said, tossing it on the chaise. "Let's keep looking though."

When we finished, I carefully took Elsie's measurements, jotting them down in my notebook next to the sketch I'd done of what I had in mind for her new gown. Using the white dress and a gold sequinned skirt she no longer wore, I would create something dazzling she would want to wear for years to come; something that would make her feel like a Hollywood starlet whenever she put it on.

An elegant older woman strolled into the room. She looked like a perfect copy of Elsie except twenty-five years older. She smiled placidly at me before turning to Elsie.

"Darling, I just heard back from the Crowleys. They won't be able to attend. They already have plans to go to Brighton that weekend."

"Brighton," Elsie scoffed. "How mundane."

I rolled my measuring tape back up and put it back in my kit.

"Mother, this is Nora Archer, the seamstress I told you about. She's going to make me a stunning new dress," Elsie said in the tone reserved for those used to making introductions between important people in society. "Nora, this is my mother, Caroline Foster-Quinn."

She reached out her gloved hand and I shook it with my naked one.

"Pleasure, dear," she said. "Elsie told me she also purchased some stockings from you?"

A strangled chuckle escaped my throat. "Yes, that's correct."

"Where did you get them?" Her face read innocence but her tone was all suspicion.

To be fair, she had a right to be suspicious of me. I *had* sold her daughter black-market goods. On the other hand, her daughter knowingly purchased black-market goods *from* me.

"I am not at liberty to discuss that," I said, friendly but firm.

Mrs. Foster-Quinn spotted my notebook on the chaise and inspected the sketch, her eyes then roaming to the two garments laying nearby.

"What do you think, Mum? I think it will be so chic."

The glow on Elsie's face gave me a thrill. She believed in me. Someone who obviously had good taste and money to burn believed I could create something beautiful for her. It gave me hope.

"Yes," Mrs. Foster-Quinn said slowly. "That will be quite lovely." She pursed her lips slightly. "Do you have time to do a second gown before then?"

Since it was already nearly evening, I made an appointment to come back and survey her closet as well. Between my current roster of clients, Elsie's dress and her mother's gown, I knew I would be putting in a lot of hours in the next couple of weeks.

Mrs. Foster-Quinn showed me out, suddenly warming to me despite my illicit criminal activity.

"Are you sure you don't want a lift home? I can have our driver come pick you up in a few minutes."

"No, no. I am perfectly happy to take the bus," I said as I made for the front door, my heels clicking on the marble floors of their grand lobby. "Thank you though—"

"You sound like my son," she scoffed. "Oh, there he is now."

I turned to see Jack, wide-eyed, staring at me from the doorway. "What are you doing here?"

My stomach dropped and my mouth hung open. This was *his* family home? This was *his* family?

"Goodness, Jack," Mrs. Foster-Quinn scolded. "I'm sorry, Miss Archer. He's not usually so ill-mannered—"

"It's alright," I said, snapping my mouth shut and straightening, composing myself. "We know one another. I just didn't realize he was your son."

She tilted her head slightly. "Oh. You know one another. Small world." She excused herself to check on dinner, leaving Jack and I alone in the elegant entryway.

I turned to him, my eyes still wide. "You are full of surprises."

He nodded for me to follow him through the house and out a back door. Jack didn't seem to notice my astonishment at the splendour of their garden—topiaries, a fountain, a fish pond, trees, and flowers of every color stretched out before us, all contained by a high stone wall. There was a lovely little bench nearby but Jack didn't suggest I take a seat.

"To answer your question, I'm sewing a dress for your sister for an upcoming event and now I'm apparently making one for your mother too," I explained.

"How on earth did you meet Elsie?"

"She came into the shop. Her friend recommended my services."

I didn't mention the stockings. The fewer people who knew about them, the better.

Jack glanced at me before crossing his arms over his chest, his face still tight.

"Are you…annoyed with me?"

His expression eased and he dropped his arms to his sides. "Of course not."

"You've been acting so strangely since this morning. I thought…I thought we had fun on Saturday."

"We did."

"Then why are you trying so hard not to look at me?"

Jack's eyes finally found mine. He parted his lips slightly to speak, hesitated, and then cleared his throat. "I realized I might be coming on a little strong. You're so busy with your business right now. I…I think it might be better if we remained friends for the time being." He winced ever so slightly.

A charming chap from a rich family leads a girl on and then pulls away. Where have I heard that one before?

My gut twisted but I shoved it away.

"Alright then," I said, summoning a chipper tone and taking a seat on the bench. "Tell me. Is this where you grew up?"

If I changed the subject, perhaps it would hide the hurt in my voice. *How did I misread him so badly?*

Jack let out a long breath. "Yes." He joined me on the bench. "My mother and I lived in Islington until my father died and my mother remarried."

"That's why you're a Parker and not a Foster-Quinn."

He rolled his eyes. "My stepfather insisted I stay a Parker. He has never run out of ways to remind me I'm not his real son."

"Wow," I said. "That's cruel."

"I make him sound like a monster. I shouldn't. He sent me to the best schools and gave me so many opportunities I wouldn't have had otherwise and I'm grateful for that." He glanced at me. "Archie, my younger half brother, he's the favorite. He's the one who'll carry on the family name and take over the family business."

"But's that good, isn't it? That means you can stick with your—" I made my voice sound a bit snooty "—academic pursuits."

Jack smiled wide, his body relaxing a bit. "Yes, that's true." His smile quickly faded. "Unless he doesn't come back."

He told me about receiving word about his brother's capture while serving overseas. My three younger brothers worked in reserved occupations on the docks and were relatively safe so I couldn't imagine how Jack must have felt.

"I feel so guilty for feeling afraid for my own future when I should only be worried about his safety," he said, staring straight ahead. "I must sound like a git."

"No. You don't," I said softly. "You can be worried about two things at once. It's okay."

I reached over and placed my palm on his hand, if only to give him something resembling comfort. Perhaps I shouldn't have. He just looked so bloody sad.

Jack, still looking out into the garden, turned his hand over and entwined his fingers with mine. He looked down at our hands, the corner of his mouth curving into a small smile. His gaze trailed from my fingers, along my arm, across my chest and up my neck, landing on my lips. He dragged his eyes up to meet mine.

"That event my sister mentioned," he said, "would you have any interest in coming?"

Startled, I laughed. "What?"

"To the fundraiser," he clarified. "You should come as my date."

"Your date who is just your friend?"

We glanced down at our hands, still clasped together between us, and simultaneous separated them.

"Yes," he said, his inflection going up at the end like it was a question.

"Your sister didn't make it sound like a good time."

"Oh, I never said it would be a good time." He chuckled. "But you should still come."

"Why?"

His brows raised. "Why?"

"Yes. Why do you want me there? Why should I be your friend-date?"

He blinked a few times as he considered his response. "It would be more enjoyable if you were there."

"And?"

"Aaand it could be a good business opportunity for you. There will be quite a few wealthy people in attendance who could become your clients." He thought quickly. "There will also be a few well-off bachelors there. How do you feel about marrying a widower in his seventies?"

I gave him a playful slap on the arm. "You're terrible."

"Perhaps," he said, a gleam in his eye. "You should come with me anyway."

"Will there be champagne?"

"Loads."

I sighed. "Fine, I'll be there. Rich old ladies could very well be my bread and butter."

Jack was beckoned to dinner with his family and I finally made it to the bus stop.

While I waited I considered how strange Jack was. He seemed to have feelings for me and yet…and yet he wanted to keep his distance.

I silently hoped I had not fallen prey to a privileged man's games.

Again.

ten

JACK

———— ❖ ————

I didn't see much of Nora for the next few weeks. The dress she made for Elsie was enough work to keep her busy, but then she had my mother's dress *and* her existing client base on top of that. If I wanted to steal a glimpse of her at all, I had to get up very early to catch her on her way to the bus or stay up very late. I was convinced she slept at the shop some nights.

I got my hair trimmed and finished getting ready at my parents' house in St John's Wood and Nora would meet me downstairs before dinner.

Elsie spun around in front of the mirror, admiring her new Grecian-style gown with a glittering gold V-shaped cluster of handsewn sequins, beads, and embroidery at the bust.

"Nora is a genius," Elsie said, turning again. "I can't believe she made this from old clothes I wasn't wearing anymore. I must hire her again."

I fussed with my bow tie in front of the mirror. "She's very talented."

Elsie, hand on her hip, made eye contact with me in the mirror. "Mum said you two know one another somehow?"

"I rent her aunt's garret," I said plainly, "and Nora has lived there since last year when she was bombed out."

I could tell Elsie was barely listening at this point, too busy making eyes at her own reflection. She took a seat at her vanity and pursed her lips as she tried to decide what earrings to wear.

"I suppose Mother has you seated beside Lucinda Pope, as usual," she said. "At least talk to the poor girl this time."

My mother had been trying to shove Miss Pope and I together for several years. Her uncle was a baronet and had connections in Parliament. I expect Mother and Father wanted us paired up to help my stepfather's not-so-secret political ambitions.

"I expect I will be seated beside my date."

Elsie turned in her chair. "Your date?" She let out a surprised chuckle. "Who is your date?"

I slid my arms into my tuxedo jacket. "Miss Archer."

My sister shook her head. "Who?"

I shot her a look over my shoulder. "You have met her several times and you don't even remember her name? You literally just said she was a genius. Nora. Nora is my date tonight."

Elsie's eyes widened. "Nora is your date? Nora, as in the seamstress?"

"Yes, Elsabeth, Nora the seamstress."

I only used her full name when I was annoyed with her. I used it quite often.

She stood and stared at me. "Does Mum know?"

"Not yet."

"Are you trying to give her a heart attack?"

I rolled my eyes. "Why must you be so dramatic?"

"If you didn't think it was going to be a problem, you would have told Mum already."

I looked back to the mirror as I adjusted my cuffs. She was perhaps correct on that account.

"Don't worry," I said. "I'll make sure she uses the flatware when she eats instead of just putting her face directly onto the plate."

"Why did you invite..." Elsie's expression hardened. "You don't have feelings for this woman, do you?"

Despite trying to get over my little fixation, seeing less of Nora made me yearn for her somehow even more.

"If I did it would be none of your concern, Elsie."

"Oh, my god. You do. You *like* her." Her eyes were bright as she joined me by the mirror. "Oh, this is so scandalous."

"I'm a school teacher, not a duke." I turned to leave her dressing room, feeling anxiety creeping up my neck.

"And how does the lady feel about you?"

"I'm too far away to hear your invasive question. So sorry!" I called back to her as I fled before she asked me anything else.

Besides, I wasn't actually sure how Nora felt. When I told her we should only be friends, she barely seemed affected at all. It seemed like saying the words pained me far more than it bothered her to receive them.

I hoped I might have a better idea of her feelings by the end of the night.

Guests began arriving right on time and—as Elsie predicted—they were mostly in their fifties and sixties.

"It's for charity," Elsie reminded me, spotting my grimace.

Mum glided down to the lobby. She shimmered in the gown Nora made for her; a cream dress with green leaves embroidered around the skirt like crawling vines. Mrs. Garnier, one of her high society friends, gasped when she saw it.

"What a stunning gown, Caroline. You have such excellent taste."

Mum preened, not bothering to credit Nora for her hard work. Mrs. Garnier gave a little wave to Elsie and I as we stood together off to the side along with her date, Percy.

For the twenty-seventh time that evening I glanced at the front door.

"Oh, dear," Elsie said from beside me. "You've got it *bad*."

"Oh, do be quiet."

"Elsie told me about your little crush," Percy said, amused.

I slowly turned to send a glare her way. "Can you perhaps not—"

"Oh, hush," she said, her eyes darting to the door and then back again. "Try not to look back too eagerly but she just arrived." Elsie suddenly erupted with laughter. "Oh, Jack," she exclaimed at a ridiculous volume. "You really are *so* funny. Such a wit."

I rolled my eyes and turned to see Nora. Statuesque and perfect, her sleek floor-length cobalt blue gown shimmered as she stepped closer to us. A fine gold chain bracelet graced both wrists and her lovely throat, resting at her clavicle. The neckline plunged into a deep V, landing in between her breasts and I caught a glimpse of her stockings through the slit in the front of her skirt as she walked. Her thick golden waves, kept long, framed her face and rested on her shoulders.

I stared at her. I couldn't help it. Nora was always stylish and very put together but she just looked so glamorous and majestic. Feeling a joyful grin spreading across my face as she joined us, I completely forgot anyone else was there.

"Good evening, Jack." Her chandelier earrings sparkled as she tilted her chin up to smile sweetly at me with brilliant cherry red lips.

"Hello," I said.

Elsie poked her head out from beside me. "Hello, Nora. Lovely to see you again. Everyone seems so impressed with my gown and with Mum's. You did wonderful work."

"Nice to see you too," Nora said, seeming shy. "And thank you."

"You look…" The right words would not come. Every word or phrase that came to mind didn't do her justice. "Dazzling," I finally said.

"Thank you." Nora smirked. "You're looking quite distinguished, professor."

And then the two of us just sort of stood there smiling at one another until Elsie, apparently, felt uncomfortable and cut in.

"This is my friend, Percy. Percy, this is Nora Archer," she said quickly. "She is brilliant."

They exchanged a polite head nod.

"Did you make this too?" Elsie gestured to Nora's deep blue gown. "It's stunning."

"I did," Nora said. "Thank you so much for saying that."

Percy's eyes hardened as he looked at the front door. "Who invited *him*?"

We all turned to see Warren Denning enter, his dim wife Helen on his arm.

"Must have been my parents," I scoffed. "Let's hope he's not seated near us at dinner."

As I lifted my arm, offering it to Nora, I caught her staring at Denning, her eyes wide, her jaw set and her breath quick.

"Are you alright?" I whispered.

Nora tore her eyes from Denning as if I had broken her trance. Smiling weakly she nodded stiffly and slid her hand under my arm.

She knows Denning. How does she know that blighter?

My mother, assuming all the younger party attendees would want to socialize together instead of mingling with the older ones, seated Nora, Elsie, Percy and I at the same end of the table as Denning and Helen. In fact, Helen was directly to my right and Denning to the right of her.

When Nora noticed, her eyes went wide again before she quickly lowered them. She reached for her water glass with an unsteady hand.

"Are you alright?" I whispered.

"I'm fine," she replied far too quickly.

"Are you sure?"

She nodded, gripping her water glass so tight I thought it might crack.

"Parker. Good to see, old chap," Denning said, leaning around his wife to talk to me. "I thought I heard you'd volunteered for the war effort. I'm surprised to see you here."

"I *did* volunteer," I explained. "The powers that be decided I would be more useful teaching history at a grammar school than messing about on the front lines."

Denning laughed, the volume and sound of his chuckle obnoxious. "You're joking! You're serving your country by babysitting a bunch of brats all day? That sounds bloody awful."

I narrowed my eyes at him. "There's more to it than that—"

"I think I'd rather be shot at." Denning laughed again.

I think I'd rather you be shot at, too.

"What about you? Why aren't you in uniform?"

I shouldn't have asked.

"Father made sure I got a job at the War Office," he said. "What's the point of knowing people who know people if they can't get you out of a sticky situation like conscription?"

Nora's eyes narrowed as she put her water glass back. I watched as she squeezed her hands into fists in her lap until the knuckles turned white.

"Well," I said to Denning, "you're lucky."

"Your brother is serving, isn't he? I'm surprised your father didn't get him out of it."

Across from me, Elsie glared at Denning. "Archie was proud to do his duty for his country," she said.

"Ah, yes. He does seem the type, doesn't he? How is he doing?"

Elsie and I exchanged glances.

"He's fine," Elsie replied quickly, turning her attention to Denning's wife. "Helen, I love your dress. That color is so pretty on you."

"Thank you so much," Helen said vacantly. "Your dress is lovely too."

"Oh, thank you. It's made from two pieces of clothing I wasn't even wearing anymore," Elsie said. "Jack's companion, Nora, sewed it."

Nora, usually so confident, recoiled a bit at the sound of her name. She smiled reluctantly as Helen peered around me to see the stranger in question. After Helen made her polite greeting and sat back, Denning took a quick look. An unmistakable expression of recognition flickered over his face and he quickly sat back without saying hello.

They *did* know one another. And they evidently had not parted on friendly terms.

Not that I would have expected Nora to put up with Warren Denning's insolence and obnoxious behavior.

Dinner was soon served and, thankfully, conversations changed direction. At least Denning had gone quiet. I wondered if Nora's presence had anything to do with that.

"This is delicious," Nora said from beside me. It was the first thing she uttered besides shy greetings since we sat down. "Your mum is a fantastic cook."

"Oh. Uh, my mother doesn't..." I felt my mouth twist in amusement. "You're messing me about."

She grinned. "Of course."

"I believe the vegetables were grown in our own gardens," I said.

Nora tilted her head slightly. "Oh. I didn't notice any vegetable plots when we were in the garden a few weeks ago."

"No, not this garden," I said without thinking. "I meant our gardens at our—" *Oh, hell.* "—other house."

She arched an eyebrow, amused. "The *other* house?"

"It's in Suffolk," Elsie cut in. "Jack, you should take Nora sometime. It's so beautiful out there. It's not far from the shore."

The image of Nora and I splashing in the salty sea foam appeared in my mind and I yearned to take her there that very instant, leaving this stupid party and everyone else there.

"It sounds lovely," she said, not committing to anything.

I forced the disappointment away, suddenly remembering we were attending the party as friends and nothing more.

eleven

Nora

———⋇———

I need to get out of here.

My blood ran cold as soon as I laid eyes on Warren Denning, his pretty dark-haired wife on his arm.

Not that I still had any type of romantic feelings towards him now. Nothing like that. The man I fell for wasn't real. The man I fell for was an illusion brought to life by a serial philanderer and stupid girl who wanted a different life and thought a rich man could make that happen for her.

When Warren's eyes met mine at the dinner table, my stomach twisted and turned. My skin burned with hate and every word that came out of his mouth felt like poison dripping into my ears.

Our plates were cleared away and cocktails and champagne flowed freely. I stood at Jack's side, his dutiful date, as he chatted with his sister's date, Percy. Warren kept stealing glances at me from the bar. With each tumbler of liquor he swallowed, his looks my way became longer and less inhibited. I kept my eyes on the floor but I could tell he was still surveying me from a distance. I could still feel his eyes crawling across my skin like he still had a right to it.

I tried to control my breaths but it was like my lungs couldn't quite fill.

Why did I even come tonight? Why am I even here?

The dull hum of small talk droned in my ears. I watched as old, rich friends socialized with old, rich friends. These people didn't want a sales pitch from me—some intruder into their exclusive club. They wanted to talk about the good old days and congratulate each other on succeeding in inheriting wealth. I had no business being there.

The oxygen grew thinner. I looked up at Jack, his jaw already speckled with beard growth. He looked incredible and somehow natural and effortless in his perfectly tailored tux. I wondered if he was simply born wearing one. He was handsome on any normal day but put the man in a tuxedo and he was the most dashing man I'd ever seen.

Oh, yes. That's why I'm here. Right. That makes sense.

"Are you feeling alright? You look a little flushed," he said, his hand on my arm.

"I'm a little warm," I said. "I think I'll nip out to the garden for some fresh air."

He offered me his arm again and we slipped out together. I wondered if something as benign as sitting alone together in the garden would cause a scandal to these people.

I gulped in the cool air outside and took a seat on the bench, watching the cherubs in the fountain spit water out of their mouths.

How is that *considered elegant?*

"How does your family know Warren Denning?" I let my eyes settle on the fountain. I wasn't ready to talk about this while meeting Jack's disappointed gaze.

"His father is friends with my stepfather," he explained. "Warren Denning is a tosser and none of us like him. We mostly just feel bad for his wife."

I snickered.

With his hands in his trouser pockets, Jack took a seat beside me on the bench.

"And how do you know him?"

I swallowed and tilted my chin up as anxiety wrapped its fingers around my throat. "He is my biggest regret."

Jack didn't pressure me to say more. He let the words linger between us.

"I thought he was going to marry me," I said after a long silence. "I'd never met anyone like him before and he wanted me. He was charming and generous. It was all an act and I fell for it. He talked about plans for the future so I…I didn't see the harm in…acting like a wife to him."

I silently hoped Jack knew what I meant without me having to spell it out for him. Jack's expression didn't change however. He just sat listening, letting me get everything out.

"And then I learned about his fiancée. He was engaged to Helen the entire time," I continued. "When I confronted him he acted like I was a fool for thinking someone like him would marry someone like me. He laughed at me. *Laughed* at me. I went home that night and my mother wanted to know why I was so upset so I told her everything. Everything I'd done." I inhaled deeply and let out a long breath. I really didn't want to ruin my makeup with tears. "She put me out of the house and Gloria took me in. I lived with them for a few months and then moved to Barnaby Street after that."

Jack was silent, keeping his gaze on the fountain in front of us. He tented his fingers as he considered. Eventually, he sat back on the bench and sighed.

"If I were to kill Denning, would you rather I use an antique sword or an antique pistol? Because my stepfather has one of each. I don't know how to use either but I'd be willing to give it a try if you asked me to."

A surprised laugh escaped me. "You don't need to defend my honour."

"I don't *need* to, no, but I think I would very much enjoy running him through with a sabre." He finally turned to look at me. "Thank you for telling me."

"I was young and naïve," I said with a small shrug. "I hope you don't think less of me now."

Jack's brows met in the middle. "Of course not." He turned his body towards me on the bench. "No, I—" His hand lifted, like he was going to reach for me, but then he withdrew. "No, I don't think less of you. Not in the slightest."

I stared at his hand, desperately wishing I knew what he meant to do with it. Brush my arm? Caress my cheek? Cradle my face in his palm?

Why does he keep pulling away?

"You obviously mean a great deal to your aunt," he said. "I am trying to respect her wishes—"

"Her wishes? What wishes? What did Gloria say to you?"

The corner of Jack's mouth curved up slightly and his eyes warmed. "I'm going to have to find somewhere else to live."

"What do you—"

"Jack! There you are," Elsie called from the door out to the garden. "There's a photographer here from some newspaper or some nonsense. They want a photo of the whole family for their article about the fundraiser." She glanced to me. "Pardon the interruption."

Jack sent an apologetic glance my way and I followed the two of them inside. While the Foster-Quinn family (plus one Parker) smiled and posed, I fetched some champagne and lingered near the back of the grand room.

I felt his presence before I saw him sidle up to me. The tiny hairs on the back of my neck prickled and I forced myself to keep staring straight ahead.

Smashing my champagne flute against the wall behind me and stabbing Warren in the eye with the jagged glass also came to mind.

"Good evening, stranger," he said, his voice low and lubricated with spirits.

"Please go away."

"That is a rather rude thing to say to an old friend."

"You are *not* my friend," I said, quietly but clearly. "We were never friends. Please leave me alone."

"Oh, don't be so dramatic."

Jack spotted us from across the room but he was obviously stuck in a conversation with someone. Even from so far away, I could see him trying to cut this older gentleman off so he could get back to me but this man wasn't having it.

"I see you've found yourself another wealthy chap," he said. "Good for you. I respect a woman who knows what she wants and goes for it."

I shot him a glare and left my spot at the back of the room, desperately looking around for someone else I could talk to. Someone who Warren might not speak so candidly in front of.

Jack escaped that conversation and then got cornered by an angelic blonde woman who was clearly eager for his attention.

As I approached a group of older ladies, hoping they would let me into their little cluster, they got distracted by something and wandered away, not even noticing I was there.

I heard Warren chuckle behind me. "It's like you're a ghost."

"Stop following me," I hissed and frantically searched for a window I could throw myself out of.

"That pretty young thing Jack is chatting up is Lucinda Pope," Warren said. "She and Jack have known each other their whole lives. They're from the same world. They share a bond you could never begin to understand."

She actually belongs here. Maybe she belongs with Jack too.

"Why are you even talking to me?" I snapped louder than I meant to, startling an older couple nearby.

I smiled reluctantly at them and Warren cackled at my social faux pas as "Come Josephine in My Flying Machine" played from the other side of the room.

Downing my champagne in a single gulp, I put the flute down on a nearby table and tried to make for the door so I could get outside and away from this nightmare.

Warren stepped in my path again. "I hate to be the one to break the bad news to you but your boyfriend, the fool, doesn't make use of his family money." He took another step towards me. "I could set you up in a very nice flat in Chelsea." His eyes roamed from my feet to my hair. "I've missed your fire. Your passion."

I stared at him, my pulse pounding in my ears. "You are a pathetic excuse for a man."

"Denning," Jack said from behind me. "I believe I just heard your wife announce she's expecting."

I looked over my shoulder at Jack, relief flooding my system. His eyes were steely with no hint of congratulations or warm wishes in sight.

Warren simpered. "Yes. I was telling Miss Archer that Helen might be needing some of her clothes altered."

Jack's eyes narrowed, seeing right through Warren's obvious lies. He raised his arm and I gladly slipped my arm under it, knowing Warren would leave me alone. At least for now.

Later on in the evening, I found myself in Jack's arms, swaying to the rhythm of a slow romantic tune—the third time we'd found ourselves in such a situation.

I leaned in closer so I could whisper to him. "Earlier, what did you mean by you'll need to find another place to live?"

Jack let out a sigh, smiling softly. "Your aunt requested that I not—" He struggled to find the right words. "—pursue you while you and I both live in her home."

My shoulders dropped. "Oh. I didn't know."

"Yes, apparently we've been less than subtle with our, uh, our exchanges."

I laughed. "Our exchanges? Is that what we're calling it?"

"I didn't tell you because I don't want to cause any sort of rift between you and Mrs. Sampson. I'll find somewhere else to live." He paused. "That is, if you think I should."

"I don't want you to go. I like knowing you're just upstairs. I like seeing you at breakfast. I like seeing you at dinner," I said. "But perhaps you should."

The song ended, switching to a faster tempo jazz number. Jack held tight to my waist, our eyes locked. My neck felt hot and my breaths quickened. I slipped my hand from his and placed it on his chest so I could feel his heartbeat racing to catch up with mine.

Behind Jack, I noticed Warren watching us. He smirked when our eyes met, and I quickly turned away. Jack looked over his shoulder and automatically pulled me closer, protectively.

I donned my best posh accent, "You must know I'm having a topping time at this little soirée, Mr. Parker, but would it be at all possible for us to leave a little early and perhaps go somewhere a little more…lively?"

Jack grinned. "What did you have in mind?"

eleven

JACK

———※———

We slipped out of the house and took a cab to Soho, still in our formal wear. As we sped into central London, Nora slid her hand into mine. I lifted her hand to my lips and laid a kiss on it, causing her crimson lips to spread into a wide smile.

I was infatuated with that smile.

Nora handed some cash to the cabbie and we disembarked at the darkened street corner. I wasn't even sure where in Soho we were since England was still under a blackout order. Nora took my hand again and lead me down an alley and then knocked twice on a nondescript door. A few raindrops landed on my shoulders as we waited, and Nora held a protective hand over her hair.

When the door swung open, lively swing music flooded the alley and we made our way inside past the doorman.

"I sure hope you can dance, Parker," Nora said as I followed her down the dimly lit staircase to the basement jazz club.

I certainly knew of Soho's jazz club scene but had never visited one before. An elegant Black woman in a red gown crooned into the microphone while the band wailed behind her. Couples of all colors and shapes twisted, spun, and whirled on the busy dance floor. The room felt electric.

Sidling up to the bar, I said, "To answer your question, yes, I *can* dance. Elsie made me learn when we were younger. But I'll need some courage first." I ordered us some drinks and we drained them quickly, our competitive natures raising to the surface.

We found an empty spot on the floor and let the music take us away. Due to the combination of the warm bodies around us, the liquor, and how Nora looked in that dress, I tore my bow tie from my throat and shoved it roughly into my pocket.

Although not nearly as skilled as some of the dancers around us, we were certainly the only ones in formal fundraiser garb and it caused more than a few people to take notice. Nora and I managed to keep up with each other, spinning madly to the swinging beat. Her face glowed with joy as I twirled her around the floor, our feet moving in sync. We rested for a few minutes, quenching our thirst with a pair of martinis before getting back on the floor.

When we finally decided to call it a night, the few raindrops had turned into a downpour.

I handed my tuxedo jacket to Nora and braved the deluge to wait for a cab on the street so she could stay at least slightly dry.

I waited for a few minutes, but there were no cabs to be had. Besides the rain smacking the pavement and a few other late-night pedestrians, the street was silent.

Nora joined me on the street, my jacket over her shoulders and her stylish curls drenched and matted to her neck.

"What are you doing?" I laughed. "You're going to get soaked out here."

"It's just rain. It'll dry," she exclaimed over the pounding of the drops on the street.

I stared at her and watched as rain collected on her long eyelashes, leaving a trail of grey on her cheek before slipping off the edge of her chin.

"I really want to kiss you," I said. "Would that be alright?"

She smirked and glanced at the sky. "In this weather? On the side of the street?"

"It's just rain." I wrapped my arms around her and pulled her close. "It'll dry."

Nora clung to me as I pressed my mouth to hers and a rush of adrenaline shot through me. Our kiss tasted of cocktails and I savored every sweet note mingling between our tongues. Embracing her tighter, my hungry lips slid over hers while my body felt like it was on fire, despite the steady rain pounding down on us. Nora gave a little nibble of my bottom lip before her mouth spread into a smile. I nuzzled my dripping wet nose against hers.

"I don't often do that with my friends," she said, resting her forehead against my chin.

I chuckled, dragging my lips along her jawline. "Nor do I."

A motorcar sped by, honking their horn a moment before splashing us with cold water collecting on the street. Nora groaned loudly into the sky.

"Maybe we could find a tube station to sleep in," she suggested.

I grabbed her hand and jogged across the street. "I have a better idea."

Together we ran through the pouring rain, dashing through puddles and laughing like children. When we needed a break to catch our breaths, we duck into a telephone box. Squeezed together and panting, Nora grabbed the front of my shirt to bring me closer and kissed me hard, her fingers climbing through my sodden hair. When our lips parted we just stared at one another, our chests heaving.

There is no coming back from this.

Back out into the rain we went, my hand clasping hers tight. We finally slowed to a stop in front of the Savoy, ducking under its canopy to get out of the rain. Nora burst out laughing.

"Very funny," she said. "Did you make me run all this way for a laugh?"

I threw her a coy smile, took her hand again, and led her inside to the chic lobby with its marble columns and pristine black and white flooring. The concierge raised an eyebrow at us, the two drowned rats who wandered in off the street.

Nora pulled on my arm "Jack, don't. Let's just go—"

"Good evening," I said, approaching the counter. "I will take a room, my good man."

Nora snorted with laughter behind me.

The concierge pursed his lips. "I'm afraid that will not be possible, sir. All of our rooms are booked for the night."

Nora tugged on my arm again, still giggling.

"My stepfather is Robert Foster-Quinn. I'm Johnathan Parker. I should be on his account." I smiled confidently and fished my wallet out of my pocket to show him my identification card. "Would it be possible to check again?"

His eyes widened. "Oh. One moment." He took a third of a second to check his records. "My mistake. It appears there is one single room available. Apologies for the mix-up."

While he fiddled with his books, Nora yanked my arm again.

"Yes, darling wife?" I widened my eyes slightly to signal to her to play along.

"This is too much. We don't have to—"

"Don't worry your pretty little head about it, my precious cupcake. Papa will take care of it."

I had never called my father "Papa" in my entire life.

She looked very uncertain about this plan. Personally, I was just glad to get out of the rain.

Besides, I could tell from her wide and wandering gaze she had never stepped foot inside the elegant and exclusive Savoy Hotel before. And she deserved the best.

After an incredibly uncomfortable ride in the lift with the porter and then a nearly silent walk from the lift to the room, I shut the door and laughed again.

"Be honest," Nora said, yanking off one of her heeled shoes. "That clerk at the front desk. He thinks I'm a tart, doesn't he?"

I clamped my lips tight.

"Of course he does," she said, sliding her foot out of her other shoe.

She turned on one of the lamps and a golden glow illuminated every crease and pucker in her gown, sopping and gripping every curve of her figure.

I leaned against the lavatory doorframe as she grimaced at her reflection and tried to finger-comb her stringy, sodden locks. She dampened a tissue and patted around her eyes where her makeup was smeared.

I could've watched her for hours.

"Just so you know," I said, "I didn't plan this out or anything."

Nora arched an eyebrow. "You mean you *don't* actually control the weather?"

"Oh no, I certainly do," I responded quickly. "I actually scheduled the rain for tomorrow and the chaps in the factory mucked it up and flipped the switch hours too early."

"You should really hire women to work your weather factory," she said, tossing the mascara-soiled tissue in the bin under the sink. "They're simply more reliable."

Before she flicked the lav light off, I caught myself in the mirror— my hair was just as stringy and sodden, maybe even more so, and both my shirts were very much soaked through.

Nora and I exchanged uncomfortable looks as we both assessed the one bed in the room.

"I'll sleep on the floor," I said, "or in the bathtub maybe."

"You will not," Nora said. "You're paying for the room, you should take the bed."

"I'm not actually paying for it, my father is."

"Well, in that case, you can go sleep outside." She beamed, batted her eyelashes at me and then shrugged. "We're friends, remember? We can share the bed. It's big enough for the both of us."

My stomach somersaulted. "No, I better not."

She closed the space between us and began wordlessly unbuttoning my wet shirt. "You should hang this up so it's somewhat dry in the morning." Her eyes never rose to meet mine as she diligently worked her way down.

She backed up against the wall and watched as I untucked the shirt and slipped my arms out of the sleeves, her eyes freely roaming my bare arms.

"You should hang that up too," she said, gesturing to my undershirt.

"If you insist," I said, peeling it off over my head.

She found several hangers in the closet by the door and brought them to me, taking a moment to run a finger over my bare pectorals and over my shoulder.

"And those," she said, nodding to my trousers as her eyes darkened.

She supervised as I sat on the edge of the bed and pulled my trousers down over my legs.

"I take garment care very seriously," she said, reaching for the zipper on the side of her dress and pulling it down until she could step out of it.

My breath caught in my throat as she began unfastening her stockings from her corselette and carefully rolling them down her exquisite legs.

"Garment care is important," I whispered, my voice slightly rougher than usual.

She hung up all of our wet clothes in the lavatory before going to the window, parting the curtain slightly to look at the view of the embankment, as dark as it was with the blackout. The outlines of her exposed form were reflected in the window but if she felt shy about her nudity, she certainly didn't show it.

I carefully moved her damp hair to the side, leaving her shoulder bare for me to kiss—slowly and tenderly.

She sighed deeply and slid her hand up to my neck.

"I don't want you to move—oh, that feels nice—somewhere else."

"Do you want me to stop?"

She suddenly turned to face me and wrapped her arms around my neck, pulling us both against the window behind her, only pausing long enough to whisper, "Absolutely not."

I drowned in the unlimited bliss of her body and lips pressed to mine and I let myself slip beneath the waves of desire.

With her legs hitched around my waist, I carried her to the bed and laid her down gently, continuing my trail of kisses on her neck, along her collarbone and back up her jaw and my toes curled as I deepened our kiss. I yearned to feel every inch of her skin under my fingertips. I started with the warmest place on her body and she eagerly raised her hips in encouragement.

We fit together perfectly, Nora and I. She tipped her head back into the pillow and arched her back, a serene smile spreading across her lips as I pressed into her. Locking my mouth to hers, my hips glided between her smooth thighs and our kiss stifled her moan. She broke the kiss to gasp into my jaw, the warmth of her breath tickling the hairs on my neck. I pressed another fierce kiss to her lips—it was like I could not stop kissing her or I might die—and I felt her thighs squeeze my hips in response. I stopped for a moment to try to cement that perfect image and feeling in my memory forever.

"Are you alright?" Nora panted and reached up to palm my cheek.

"Never better," I said with a chuckle, "and I mean that entirely literally."

She giggled as I clasped her hand on my face and gently brought each of her fingertips to my lips.

Afterwards, we stayed tangled up in the sheets, fatigued and content. I dragged the pad of my thumb across her rosy bottom lip and up along her cheek as I admired her sleepy and pleased expression.

I knew I adored her that night we got lost and spent the night in the tube station together. I thought I might be in love with her when she laughed and pulled me out of the pond at Hampstead Heath. But as I watched her fall asleep on the pillow beside me, one long leg still draped over my middle, I knew for certain living without her was no longer an option.

thirteen

Nora

⚜

I woke up early and decided to take advantage of the large luxury tub in the lavatory of our hotel suite while Jack dozed. I filled the tub with hot water a bit more than Londoners were supposed to—*"There's a war on!"*—and poured two bottles of bubble bath soap under the tap.

As soon as I sank into the hot water, the negative thoughts began.

I tried to push the intrusive thoughts away. But I couldn't. I wasn't even safe in my bubble bath—The Bad Thoughts forced their way in anyway.

Knowing Jack would probably go along with whatever I asked him to, I had to consider my actions carefully. I had to focus on what was best for him in the long run, not *just* what I might want.

Wrapping myself in a plush bathrobe and my hair in a towel, I watched the foamy water swirl down the drain.

Jack, shirtless, stretched and yawned when he saw me, a big grin on his handsome face.

I slid under the sheet next to him and he pulled me into him, burying his face in the back of my neck.

"You smell so good," he mumbled against my neck, his mouth on my skin. "Like a peach."

"I had a bubble bath. It was divine."

"Should we order some breakfast up to the room?" He pecked my cheek and nuzzled his nose against my ear.

He was not making this any easier.

"Unfortunately," I said gently, "we need to get back to the house before eleven when Gloria, Harry and Marvin get back from church."

Jack went still for a moment while I rolled over to face him.

He narrowed his eyes and propped himself up on an elbow. "You want to keep this a secret then?"

"Flats you can afford in northern London are hard to come by. You said so yourself."

He frowned. He already knew where I was going with this, I could tell.

I went on. "If you leave the house, you'll have to find a flat you can't actually afford—"

"I can get the money from my family," he said. "I'm not in an impossible situation when it comes to that—"

"But you hate asking them for money and I don't want you to have to do that. Not for me, especially."

"But if moving out means we can be together, isn't it worth it?"

I smiled sweetly and touched his cheek. "You'd end up resenting me for it."

"Perhaps you could find a place closer to your shop," he suggested.

"I can't really afford that yet, not with the business just starting up," I said. "Plus, Gloria would never forgive herself, and she would end up blaming you somehow. I can't have that either."

Jack frowned. "What do we do then?"

Dragging my fingertip over his tuft of curly dark chest hair, I summoned my best confident voice. "I think we, officially, remain friends."

He opened his mouth to object, but I cut him off.

"However, perhaps we could see where this goes in a sort of… discreet way." I sent him a knowing look.

"You want to be with me," he said, "in secret."

"For now."

His shoulders relaxed. I couldn't tell if it was from relief or resignation.

"If you have a better option that doesn't involve asking your family for money, I'm open to suggestions."

His expression softened. "I have no idea how this will work but I suppose we can only try." He nodded and ducked under the sheet.

"What are you doing?" Peering under the sheet at him, I giggled.

"I don't know when we'll have a chance to do this again so I figure we better use this hotel room while we've got it." He gently parted my thighs and wiggled closer to me. "Don't you agree?"

"We really ought to get back to—oh, my god." Clamping my eyes shut, my head fell back onto the pillow, my toes curled and my chest heaved. "Oh, you make a very good point there."

On the train to north London I rested my head on Jack's shoulder. He laced his fingers in between mine. It was still early for a Sunday morning so we nearly had the car to ourselves. Several other passengers *had* given us some interesting looks at the station though—a young couple in a tuxedo and a fancy frock, still visibly damp from the night before.

Yes, I'm sure we looked slightly suspicious.

I looked up at Jack. "Where did you learn to do that?"

"To do what?" He smiled smugly.

I shot him a look. "You know what."

"I had a girlfriend when I was a student at Cambridge," he said. "She was lovely. Not as lovely as you, I might add."

I beamed.

"We were together for maybe a year and a half before she found out one of my mates—a chap she didn't even talk to—was the son of an earl and suddenly I was yesterday's news, and they were inseparable."

"Oh, that's rotten," I said. "What a trollop."

"It was a long time ago. My wounded heart has healed."

I put my head back on his shoulder and closed my eyes. "I'm glad."

After a few minutes he added, "One would think I would be used to being second choice."

I looked up at him again. "Are you talking about your brother?"

He shook his head. "I shouldn't have said that."

"Is that how you feel? In your family?"

"Sometimes." He let out a small chuckle and pulled his crumpled bow tie from his pocket, smoothing its deep creases between his fingers. "You don't know Archie. He makes everything look so easy. Everyone adores him the moment they meet him." He glanced down at me. "Even if he manages to make it back, you are *never* meeting him." He winced. "Christ, what is wrong with me?"

I gave him a peck on the cheek. "Nothing. And he *will* come back."

"You don't know that."

"If he makes everything look so easy, he'll make getting back look easy, too." I looked up at him through my eyelashes and put my head back on his shoulder. "You'll see."

I transferred to a bus to go to Highgate while Jack went west to St John's Wood to see his parents. He disappeared the night before without saying goodbye, so he figured he likely owed them at least a short visit. He could change out of his tux there. Besides, it was better if we arrived back home separately.

I *just* made it into the house and upstairs to my bedroom when I heard my aunt, uncle, and cousin return home from church. I put my back to the door as I heard them begin their ascent up the stairs.

"Did you see Betsy's hat? I know we're supposed to be making do with our clothing but that thing looked like it should be burned," Gloria scoffed. "And did you see James? He doesn't look well at *all*. He's so thin now. He says it's only the food rationing. I say it's more that he's scared to go see a doctor. And did you see…"

She stopped speaking suddenly and her shadow appeared in the crack under my door.

She rapped on it. "Nora, are you in there?"

I kept my back to it to make sure she didn't come in. "Yes, I'm just getting changed."

Looking down at my gown, I winced. The damp fabric still clung in places and I didn't have any makeup on. I knew she would have questions if she saw me in that state.

I heard Harry and Marvin continue down the hall to their bedrooms while Gloria lingered at my door.

"Where were you last night? Jack didn't get home either." She lowered her voice to a stage whisper. "You two weren't together, were you?"

A surprised laugh jumped out of my throat and I instantly fought the urge to wince. *Why did I do that?* "Of course not. I mean, we were both at his parents' house for the night. A lot of the guests stayed, actually. It wasn't my original plan to stay the night but Elsie, my client, invited me to stay so I did. They have so many guest bedrooms, you know. Probably a hundred. Well, obviously not a hundred, that would be absurd. Maybe around fifteen? Actually, that seems too high, too. Maybe ask Jack when he gets home. Unless he's already home. I have no idea."

What is happening to me?

"Oh," Gloria said. "Alright. Do you have to go into the shop today or can you join us for lunch?"

"Uh, I might have to go to the shop later this afternoon but yes, lunch sounds lovely. I'll be out in a few minutes."

"Okay, dear."

As soon as I heard her amble off to her bedroom, I tipped my head back and rested it on the door, letting out a long sigh.

I had to get ahold of myself and I had to do it fast.

By the following Tuesday my nerves had eased slightly. Jack's calmness around Gloria helped me to regain composure. I was more than ready for my regular routine to get back on track.

I unlocked the front door of my shop, wiggled the key just so in that very particular way it required, and checked my schedule for that day. And then the nerves returned, somehow even worse than before.

I had completely forgotten I was to see Jack's mother that afternoon in St John's Wood. She wanted me to redo one of her old outfits and update the style of it. She suggested I have a look through her dressing room a second time—apparently similar to the one just off Elsie's bedroom—and see if there was anything else I could adapt. I loved the work and the challenge but the travel time was eating into my actual work time. If they weren't paying extra for the travel time, I would really reconsider having them as clients.

So, once again, I took the train to St John's Wood. It was like a different world in that opulent neighborhood, so close to Regent's Park. Like Hampstead Heath, Regent's Park's beautiful green was given over to military training grounds, vegetable gardens, and anti-aircraft guns. It was so disheartening.

Although the house's grandness was still a bit jarring, I'd visited the Foster-Quinn home several times so I was mostly over my starry-eyed astonishment.

Mostly.

"Good afternoon, George," I said as he opened the front door for me. "How are you today?"

"Good afternoon, Miss Archer. I am well," he said in a low, steady albeit slightly surprised tone. I realized perhaps he did not get asked about himself often. "Mrs. Foster-Quinn is waiting for you in her upstairs sitting room."

"Not to be confused with her downstairs sitting room?" I smirked at him.

"Correct," he said flatly, stoic as ever. "Down the hall on your right. It's the second door on the left."

Narrowing my eyes at him to see if he was joking, I quickly realized George had never told a joke before in his life.

"Right, okay. I'll just go upstairs then. Thank you, George."

Mrs. Foster-Quinn rose when I entered the room. "Sweet girl. Have some tea with us before we get started, won't you? This is one of my dearest friends, Mrs. Pope. Martha, this is Miss Archer, the seamstress I told you about."

Her companion nodded at me stiffly. "Hello. I've heard you're quite the talent."

"Thank you," I said, a little too much surprise in my voice. "I'm pleased my work has been so appreciated."

"Please, have a seat," Mrs. Foster-Quinn said, gesturing to a chair that looked to be from the previous century.

As I sat, I realized every piece of furniture in the room was probably over a hundred years old. Floral paintings and portraits, all in gilded frames, hung on every wall and a bountiful and professionally arranged bouquet stood on nearly every surface around the room.

Mrs. Foster-Quinn handed me a cup of tea and I sipped it as delicately as I could. I decided if I spilled the tea on this very expensive chair, I would simply leap out of the wide window on the other side of the room.

"I was just telling Mrs. Pope about Jack's war work as a teacher at the grammar school in Highgate," Mrs. Foster-Quinn said. "I don't think it's what he had in mind when he signed up but at least he's safe." A sadness appeared in her eyes as she uttered the word "safe".

I wondered if there was ever a moment in her day she didn't worry for Archie's safety.

Mrs. Pope's smile was tight. "I do worry about his finances. My Lucinda says he lives on his own income alone."

Maybe mind your own business?

"Oh, there's no need to be concerned," Mrs. Foster-Quinn said. "Robert and I will of course provide for Jack and Lucinda once they marry. I would never expect Lucinda to manage a home on an academic's salary."

My jaw clenched, I slowly lowered my tea cup and saucer to my lap. My throat went dry and my chest squeezed until I could barely breathe.

He's engaged to someone else. I fell for it again.

fourteen

JACK

At dinner on Tuesday night I knew something was wrong.

Mealtimes with the Sampsons were traditionally when Nora and I would exchange glances and secret smiles across the table. On Tuesday evening, she just stared down at her plate of food, slowly picking at it while Marvin rambled about his most recent animal discoveries—a fairly common event at their dinner table.

"Did you know there is a type of frog you can see some of his insides because part of him is see-through? It's called a glass frog and it lives in South America."

Mrs. Sampson wrinkled her nose.

"And then there's another frog that lives in Asia that looks like he's covered in moss. It helps to protect him from predators."

"Oh, wow," Mr. Sampson said, his eyes glazed over.

"You sure do love animals," I said.

"I think I would like to be a veterinarian. I would like to help animals." Marvin thought for a moment. "But then I would probably only get to help cows and sheep and horses."

"Maybe you could be a researcher and discover new animal

species," I said. "You could have adventures in fantastic places all over the world for science."

Marvin's face lit up. "Really? Is that a real job?"

"I think so," I said. "I'm not a scientist but I worked as a researcher before I became a teacher. No adventures through jungles or rain forests for me though."

I glanced at Nora. Her eyes remained down.

"I'm sure there are still animal species to be found here in Britain," Mrs. Sampson added, sending me a subtle warning glance.

"But the best animals are in South America and Asia and Africa," Marvin exclaimed. "Britain's animals are so dull."

"They're not so bad," Mr. Sampson mumbled. "Sheep are plenty interesting."

Mrs. Sampson chuckled. "What on earth would *you* know about sheep?"

He turned his attention to his wife, his expression detached as ever. "They're quite woolly."

"When I lived in the country during the evacuation, there were a bunch of farms so there were lots of sheep and cows and horses and they weren't interesting at all." Marvin shrugged. "They had a nice dog though. It was a Border Collie and he could run so fast. I guess helping dogs as an animal doctor would be alright. I like dogs."

I smiled weakly, thinking about Marvin being sent off to the country before the war started. He was probably terrified. Mrs. Sampson was likely beside herself with worry. All London children were supposed to leave but there were enough left for me to be put on teaching duty.

What parent in their right mind would keep their child in London when the Germans were expected to drop bombs or gas attack us at any moment? The parents and guardians of my pupils, that's who. It was yet another reason I resented my teaching job.

Some parents, like the Sampsons, chose to bring their young ones back early, deeming London safe enough. When he came back, I tutored him so he could get caught up to his classmates since his country schoolhouse education was quite lacking compared to the rigours of Highgate Grammar School.

"Did you like it in the country?" I asked.

"It was okay." Marvin shrugged again. "It would have been better if they had see-through frogs though."

After dinner Nora threw me a glance and then left the house. Keeping a safe distance, I followed her to a small park not far from her aunt's house. As soon as she felt we were far enough away she whipped around and glared at me, her eyes cold as ice and her hands curled into fists at her sides.

I stopped in my tracks. "You did want me to follow, right?"

"Yes," she snapped.

I arched an eyebrow. "Did I do something wrong?"

Nora's eyes narrowed as she stepped closer to me.

"Lucinda Pope," she said slowly, jaw clenched.

"What about her?"

She shook her head at me from across the stretch of park green between us. "You're no better than Warren. I can't believe I fell for it *again*. I must be the most gullible idiot in the entire—"

"Nora, what are you talking about?"

"You're engaged to Lucinda Pope."

I blinked at her. "That is certainly news to me."

"Don't bother pretending," she scoffed. "I went to see your mother because she wants me to work on something for her and Mrs. Pope was there and the two of them were discussing your upcoming nuptials and how your parents are going to give you money once you and Lucinda are settled and how everything is all planned out."

I closed my eyes and sighed at the sky. "Good lord, Nora. I am absolutely not engaged."

When I opened my eyes Nora was still glaring at me, her arms crossed over her chest.

I continued. "I have never been engaged to anyone, certainly not Lucinda Pope. I haven't even been on a date with her because I have never had any sort of romantic feelings for her."

"Then why would—"

"Because my mother thinks me marrying Lucinda Pope would help my stepfather's political career after the war. It's absurd and I have explained this to my mother on several occasions."

"But she's lovely and you've known one another forever," Nora said. "She's part of your world while I might as well be from another planet. I saw her at the fundraiser so I know how pretty she is—"

"You *did* see her at the fundraiser," I interjected. "You saw her because you were there *with me*. Do you really think if I were actually engaged to Lucinda that I would have shown up to that party with you as my date?"

Nora's face softened and her hands unclenched. "Why would they be talking about you two getting married? I don't understand."

I rolled my eyes. "Because Lucinda has always had a bit of a crush on me. It's nothing, I promise."

After a long moment, Nora rubbed the spot on her forehead between her eyes. "I must sound insane."

"Maybe a little." I closed the distance between us. "I'll be honest though. I'm flattered."

"What?"

"I think you fancy me quite a bit," I said.

"I do not. I basically despise you." She grinned. "*You're* the one who is obsessed with *me*."

She wasn't entirely wrong.

I leaned in and laid a gentle kiss on her lips. When she returned it with eagerness, I wrapped my arms around her middle as her hands glided up my chest to rest on my neck. Joy and relief surged through me as the ardor between our bodies intensified.

She pulled her mouth away from mine and she touched her nose to my cheek. "We probably shouldn't do this in a park."

"Perhaps not," I said, tipping her chin up and kissing her softly again.

Nora opened her eyes and gazed up at me so tenderly I could have melted on the spot.

Suddenly she caught sight of something behind me and hastily backed away, her eyes wide.

I threw a glance over my shoulder and caught a glimpse of Marvin taking off on his bicycle.

Nora put her hand over her eyes. "Oh, god. He saw us."

I tore after him, running as fast as I could to catch up to him. Thankfully he was cycling away from his house and, also fortunately, was not a fast rider.

Panting like mad, I shouted, "Marvin, please stop!"

He braked and looked back at me, a deep crease between his eyes and his mouth twisted with confusion. I rested my hands on my thighs as I panted.

"I'm sorry you saw that," I said between gulps of air. "You weren't supposed to see that."

Nora caught up with us, her face painted with worry.

I approached Marvin like one might approach a skittish cat, holding my hands out in front of me and keeping my voice calm, despite the nervous panic I felt in my stomach.

Marvin's frowned deepened as he saw Nora behind me. He looked back at me and stayed silent, studying my guilty expression.

That's the point where I wasn't exactly sure how to explain this to a twelve-year-old.

"Marvin, darling," Nora began, "Mr. Parker and I have feelings for one another." She smiled sweetly at me and held my hand. "We've been keeping it a secret. And now you know."

Marvin's face softened a little. Every kid liked being in on adult-type secrets. "Why is it a secret?"

I swallowed. "Well, uh, because…" I looked to Nora.

"Because your mum and dad can't know," she said, her tone friendly but firm. "Since we both live in the same house, it wouldn't be, uh, proper for us to be dating while living together."

I couldn't help but crack a smile when she said "dating."

"Would Mum be mad if she knew?" Marvin studied the chrome on his bike's handlebars.

Nora nodded. "Probably. She would make Mr. Parker leave and find another place to live and that's really hard right now because so many homes were hit by bombs."

Appealing to Marvin's obvious affection for me was a clever choice.

He considered this for a second and then looked between the two of us. "Are you getting married?"

The surprised guffaw that erupted from Nora's mouth nearly made me jump. Marvin stared at her.

She clamped her lips shut and cleared her throat. "No, we're not getting married." She and I exchanged glances and she rapidly explained, "I mean, not any time soon. We haven't been, er, courting long enough to consider something like that. I suppose we certainly could have that type of conversation in the future but it's far too soon for something like that. Some people may feel comfortable jumping into marriage because of the war but there is so much to consider before making that kind of decision—something that affects the rest of your life."

I raised an eyebrow at her sudden uneasy rambling. She winced.

Clearing her throat again, she looked back at Marvin. "No, we're not getting married."

He nodded again.

"Are you able to keep this between us?" I bit my lip. "We like living with your family, and we don't want to upset anyone."

"But you're lying to Mum and Dad," he mumbled, "aren't you?"

A pang of shame stung my already guilty conscience. Nora and I exchanged glances again.

"Yes, we are," she said. "But this lie isn't hurting anyone. Not really. We would never do anything to hurt your parents. Or you. This is just…something that happened between us. We didn't mean for it to happen. It just did. You can't control who you have feelings for."

My arms yearned to hold her. Nora was such a tough and smart woman and of all the chaps she could be with, she chose me. I knew I couldn't let Marvin finding out end our relationship now.

"What can we do for you to keep it a secret?" I blurted.

Nora looked sideways at me. "What?"

"I can try to get you chocolate. Or comics. Or-or-or—"

"Chocolate comics?" she suggested, mocking me.

Marvin chuckled.

I tried again. "Are there any animal books I can get for you?"

I thought about asking him how much hush money I could give him but that seemed a bit much for a twelve-year-old.

His eyes lit up. "*Animals Are Like That* by Frank Buck?"

Nora cast me a silent, warning glance.

"I'll do my best," I said.

Marvin, looking uncharacteristically smug, spit into his palm and offered me his hand. "Deal?"

Nora wrinkled her nose and looked away as I spit into my palm and slapped my hand into his, shaking his in agreement.

With one final nod he peddled away towards home, leaving Nora and I on the pavement.

"So," I said with a sigh, "should I start looking for another flat tonight or wait until tomorrow?"

She groaned and wrapped her arms around me.

She rested her head on my chest and whispered, "Can you perhaps wipe your hand off on your trousers or something before you touch me?"

fifteen

Nora

———◦———

Fridays were always a bit hectic at the shop. Ladies with weekend plans always wanted their adjustments made before then so they could show off their new garment. It was a busy week anyway—I finished Mrs. Foster-Quinn's new outfit and replaced the lining of several outfits for other clients. I sent Irene a load of socks, mittens, and scarves for her to darn. I also sold about a dozen more pairs of stockings. Women were hungry for them.

Irene arrived at the shop, a sack of mended items at her side.

"Irene! Thank goodness," I said from my sewing machine. "I'll be right with you, one second."

Irene dropped the cloth bag on the front counter and beamed. "One of our neighbors volunteered to look in on Mum and Howie this afternoon so I could run some errands so I've actually got time today, for once." She looked down at the pattern pieces laid over the fabric on the counter. "I love this print." She glanced up at me. "I can pin this if you like."

Stressed, I huffed quietly as I maneuvered my fabric around a curve on my machine. "I'll get to it eventually." Sitting back in my chair, I pushed my chest out and my shoulders back until I heard a satisfying crack between my shoulder blades.

Irene winced. "You shouldn't let yourself get so sore. You'll end up with a spine like my nan's if you keep that up." She was already pinning the pattern to the fabric, getting the thin paper as close to the edge as possible so not to waste precious materials.

Standing, I stretched again, this time tilting my neck to the left and right. I plucked a bag of small items needing darning and patching from the top of a nearby shelf. I replaced it with a bag of items Irene had mended before digging around in the little drawer near the cash register and offered Irene the money.

"For the mending and the stockings I've sold," I said.

Irene, putting the pin cushion down, counted the money. "Oh, Nora. No, this is too much."

"Of course it's not," I snipped. "That's what I charge for the stuff you've mended for me—"

"But surely you would take a cut off the top of that—"

"I'd feel silly doing that since I didn't do the labor. You do good work and—"

"Nora, I don't want your charity." She counted a few bills out and thrust towards me.

"It's not charity and I'm not taking it." I shot her a stern look over my shoulder as I returned to my sewing machine.

Irene sighed at the money, deposited it into her bag, and went back to pinning the pattern.

"How are you feeling these days?" I asked from my sewing desk, nodding at her middle. Not that there was anything showing yet.

"The morning sickness is over thankfully." Irene, relieved, gave her flat belly a pat. "I get more eggs and fruit because of this one but all I want is red meat and salt."

Pregnant and nursing mothers had use of a different ration book than most adults. Clothing rationing, I knew, made no concessions for a mother's expanding belly though. That would be *another* expense for Irene to contend with soon.

I smiled cautiously. "Are your young ones home now?"

"Not yet. We're still trying to figure some things out." She lowered her eyes. "Plus I'm not sure I want them to see their father…" She hesitated. "…in his state."

"He's still angry then?" I took out a few pins and popped them into the pincushion secured to my wrist.

"It's not like he's angry at me or Mum or anyone or anything," she said, her tone going defensive. "And he's never raised a hand to me, nothin' like that. He's just angry at the entire world. Reminds me of my dad when *he* came home from the Great War."

"I'm sure he saw some horrible things. That would change anyone," I said, not really knowing what else to say. I was relieved Howie wasn't taking his anger out on his wife.

"Plus, if he ever *did* hurt me, Howie knows Eddie would kill 'im."

"Not if I got to him first," I said before starting my machine up again.

Jack, beside me at the dinner table that night, brushed my knee with the back of his index finger—under the table and out of view of the Sampsons of course. I bit the inside of my mouth as I chewed to stop myself from smiling.

All day as I sat at my sewing machine I thought of Jack and when I might get to be in his arms again. When I might get to press my lips to his again. When I might get to feel the heat of his skin on mine again.

I was disgusted with myself, truly.

Sliding my foot over to his, I nuzzled my toes against his ankle. Jack glanced at me as I carried on eating my parsnip soup, paying him no notice.

"Where is Marvin this evening?" Jack asked, lifting his water glass to his lips. "Not feeling well?"

"He's at his grandparents' house for the weekend," Harry said. "A few of his cousins are home from the country for the weekend so Marvin went too."

"They're having a big sleepover, all eight of them," Gloria added before looking at Harry. "I have no idea where your mother thinks she's going to put them all."

Harry reached for his tea cup. "I think there was mention of a tent being put up in the garden."

She rolled her eyes. "Those kids always manage to have the sniffles. I don't understand it. I know Marvin will come home sick, you just wait."

"He'll live," my uncle said dryly.

Gloria sighed at her husband before turning back to Jack and I. "Anyway, Harry and I are going out tonight to see *That Hamilton Woman*."

I tried not to choke on my mouthful of food. "Oh?"

Gloria and Harry *never* went out except for church on Sundays and the occasional visit to see Harry's parents.

Jack's response was much more casual than mine. "Vivien Leigh and Laurence Olivier, right?"

Gloria nodded. "They're such talented actors. It's been ages since I've been to the cinema," she said, eyeing Harry. I assume she pestered him to take her since the raids stopped. "Would you two like to come with us?"

Jack and I replied simultaneously and far too quickly.

"I've got a lot of marking to catch up on," he said.

"I've got a bit of a headache unfortunately," I said. "Thank you though. Perhaps next time."

I helped Gloria clear the table and Jack dried the dishes while I washed them since Gloria was upstairs getting ready to go on her big fancy date with Harry. Harry, however, was browsing the newspaper at the dinner table a few meters away.

Jack and I barely spoke. I didn't even dare look up at him in case my heart pounded even harder than it already was.

Instead, I flicked a tiny bit of warm dish water at him from the sink.

"Hey!" He laughed. "How dare you waste warm water," he said in a posh BBC voice. "Don't you know there's a war on?"

"Oh, yes. Of course. My apologies. Won't happen again." I snorted, my shoulders shuddering with giggles.

"There's a notice in the paper," Harry said, rising from the table. "They're looking for women to volunteer teaching Make Do and Mend classes. That sounds like something you would be good at, Nora."

"Me? You think *I* would be good at teaching?"

"Perhaps you should look into it," Harry added, folding the newspaper over and tossing it on the countertop next to the sink. "Might be just the thing for you."

I surveyed the advertisement with a skeptical eye. "But if I teach people to mend their own clothes, who is going to pay me to mend their clothes for them?"

"Your clients aren't the types to attend that type of class," Jack said. "I wouldn't worry about that."

"I don't really have a lot of free time right now—"

"We all have to do our bit, Nora," Harry said, ambling out to the living room. "There's a war on, you know."

I opened my mouth to reply, "And what exactly are *you* doing for the war effort?" but he had already left the dining room. Instead I pulled the plug out of the sink and eyed the newspaper as the drain gurgled.

"Maybe you should look into it." Jack finished drying a plate and slid it into a nearby cupboard. "It could be…well, I was going to say 'fun' but it probably wouldn't be fun." He thought for a moment and lifted an index finger in triumph. "Fulfilling."

"Oh? As fulfilling as *your* war job?" I smirked.

Jack narrowed his eyes at me. "Yes, something like that." Then he whipped the damp dish towel at my bum and I let out a giggly shriek.

Gloria came downstairs, giving her curls a gentle pat, a blue dress with white polka dots hugging her round hips, the white trim hitting just above the calf. It had been a long time since I'd seen my aunt done up with full makeup and date night attire.

"Oh, you look lovely," I cooed from the kitchen.

Harry appeared in the doorway. "All set?"

Gloria nodded, looking giddy as a schoolgirl.

"Have fun!" Jack called after them.

Once we heard the door close behind them, Jack turned to me slowly. "So, Miss Archer, do you have plans for this evening?"

"Nothing comes to mind, Mr. Parker. How about you?"

"Oh. I wasn't lying." He cringed and stuffed his hands into his trouser pockets. "I really *do* have a lot of marking I *have* to do tonight. It simply cannot wait until tomorrow." His grin spread across his face, making him look like the Cheshire Cat.

He stepped towards me and I put up a hand. "No, no. Your very fulfilling teaching work comes first. I suppose I'll just lounge around my bedroom. Alone. By myself. All evening," I continued, a dramatic, wistful tone to my voice. "Maybe naked. Alone—"

Cupping my face in his hands, Jack pulled me to him and pressed the most passionate, urgent, hungry kiss to my lips and I immediately weakened, clutching the front of his shirt.

I despised how desperate for him I felt but I simply could not help myself.

Dragging my lips away from his to catch my breath, I left a trail of small kisses across his jaw and down his neck. When I looked up into his eyes, I expected to see them reflected with blazing desire. But no. Jack was smiling softly and his gaze was warm and full of fondness.

Taking his hand I led him upstairs to my bedroom, stopping briefly to make sure my aunt and uncle were truly gone.

We took our time, wordlessly undressing one another, idly caressing, and counting every freckle. He pulled me into his lap and I planted my palms on his shoulders. We kept perfect time as our sighs and gentle moans grew higher and higher.

He rested his head on my heaving chest as we lay together, our legs still entwined under the blanket. I kissed the top of his head and smiled into his blond hair.

"See?" I leaned my cheek against his forehead. "I knew you liked me."

"I don't *like* you," he said.

I pulled away from him and studied his face. I wasn't panicked though. I already sensed what he was going to say. My heart knew his heart.

His face was quite serene as he spoke. "I love you."

Sliding further down in bed and cuddling closer to him, I grazed my nose against his Adam's apple. "I love you, too."

"I know."

And then I pinched him.

sixteen

JACK

—◆—

When Elsie rang me on Saturday morning, wanting to visit and do lunch, I should have declined. At the very least, I should have been suspicious.

"I can't stay out too long," I warned. "I've got essays to grade and I have to be somewhere at half one."

Elsie sipped her tea and crossed her legs under the table. "Yes, yes, I know. You're very busy and important." She waved my comment aside with a flick of her manicured hand.

"What, were Percy and the rest of your friends busy?"

She sighed. "Percy is feeling under the weather, and the girls are busy with their war volunteering jobs." She rolled her eyes.

"You might end up having to take on one of those jobs soon enough." I reached for my tea. "They're going to conscript women soon."

"I'm already doing my part for the war effort."

"Oh? And what's that?"

She widened her eyes. "I organize and host fundraisers *all* the time, Jack." She laughed and picked up the menu. "You really are a bit slow at times. To think they made you a teacher."

The little café in St John's Wood where we sat was bustling.

The weather was lovely and warm so Elsie suggested we sit outdoors and enjoy the sun and fresh air.

"That's not official war work though," I said, "and certainly not a full-time job."

"If I get conscripted, I'll have Father make a call." She tapped on the menu and contemplated. "Perhaps I'll get the chicken salad." She glanced down the street and then back at the menu. "Perhaps not. Do you know what you're getting?"

I ignored her question. "Why do you think you shouldn't have to do war work like everyone else?"

Elsie narrowed her eyes, her brows kneading together. She held up her delicate hands. "Do these look like they're made for a real job? No. They certainly don't."

I caught Elsie glancing down the street again.

"Why do you keep—"

"Lucinda, darling! It's so good to see you!" Elsie called over to her. "Why don't you join us for lunch?"

I shot Elsie a glare which went entirely ignored.

Lucinda Pope smiled shyly at me as she approached the empty seat at our table. "Hello, Jack. It's lovely to see you."

"Here, sit. We were just looking at the menus," Elsie said, thrusting her own menu at her.

My jaw began to ache from how hard I was clenching.

Lucinda delicately slid her gloves off and tucked them into her bag before wordlessly reaching for the menu. Her golden hair was flawlessly coiffed and shimmered in the sunlight. Her blue and red patterned frock was flattering on her short and slim frame.

She always reminded me of the paper dolls Elsie had as a child— too perfect, too lovely and, simply, not real. One dimensional. That was the problem.

Elsie straightened. "Goodness, what time is it?"

"Just after twelve," Lucinda said, her voice softer than a daisy petal.

Elsie slapped a palm to her chest. "I have an appointment at half twelve. I almost forgot."

"Oh?" I said, pretending not to be furious for Lucinda's sake.

"Appointment for what exactly?"

"Hair," she simpered, rose from her seat, and grabbed her bag. "Carry on you two."

I disliked the way she said "you two"—like we came as a pair.

Lucinda smiled at me and picked up the menu again.

Behind the privacy of my menu, I fumed. Elsie knew Nora and I were involved and I never saw Lucinda as a romantic prospect—nothing of the sort. She obviously planned the whole thing. However, it was clear Lucinda was in on the scheme as well.

Perhaps she's not so sweet and innocent as I thought.

Unfortunately, if I stormed off and left Lucinda at the café alone, Mum would have my head. It's not like Mum, Elsie, or especially Lucinda knew how serious I was about Nora.

Perhaps it's time they found out.

After the waiter took our orders and menus, Lucinda folded her hands in her lap and looked at me. "How is teaching?"

"It's fine," I said, plastering a fake smile on my face. "I'll be happy when this bloody stupid war is over and I can get back to Cambridge."

"What kind of work do you do there?"

"Historical research," I said. "Lots of dithering about with documents from the sixteen and seventeen hundreds."

"That sounds fascinating."

"I love it. I look forward to getting back to it someday." I nodded. "What about you? What do you do for fun?"

Feeling the tenseness in my jaw still, I really hoped my tone of voice wasn't too harsh.

"Oh, nothing important. Tell me how you became interested in history."

This was something else Lucinda did whenever we spoke. It was clear she was taught men don't actually care what women have to say but love to be peppered with questions about their interests. This lead to an extremely one-sided conversation and it was exhausting.

"Well, I suppose I read a book about Napoleon or something as a boy and—"

"Look, it's Mr. Parker."

When I heard Marvin's voice from the pavement, I turned my head so fast I thought I may have injured my neck.

"Oh, hello, Mr. Parker," Mrs. Sampson said, her arm around Marvin's shoulder.

Standing on Mrs. Sampson's other side was Nora.

She didn't look angry or shocked or upset. Wincing slightly, her lips were tight and her shoulders lowered. As soon as our eyes met, she turned to watch the nearby traffic.

"We're going to the zoo," Marvin said, practically vibrating with anticipation.

"Again," his mother added with a quick eye roll.

"Miss Pope, this is Mrs. Sampson and her son, Marvin. He's one of my students." I swallowed. "And you might already know her niece, Miss Archer. She was at the fundraising dinner last weekend."

Nora turned back at the mention of her name. "I don't think we were introduced."

"Oh. Perhaps not." I turned back to Lucinda. "Mrs. Sampson was kind enough to let out a garret bedroom after my flat was bombed. It's quite close to school so it's perfect for me." I glanced at Nora, hoping she would catch on to my true meaning. "It's all I could ever ask for."

Nora refused to make eye contact.

Lucinda smiled politely. "It is lovely to meet you. I'm Lucinda Pope. Jack and I have been friends since we were toddlers practically."

"Mum, let's go," Marvin whispered.

"Alright, alright. Goodness," Mrs. Sampson said. "So nice to meet a friend of Mr. Parker. Have a good lunch."

The three of them went strolling towards Regent's Park located a couple blocks away. I anxiously watched them, hoping Nora would at least look back at me. But she didn't.

Go after her, you fool.

But I knew I couldn't. I couldn't reveal our relationship in front of Mrs. Sampson.

Instead, I propped my elbow up on the table and rested my face in my palm and whispered a curse word into my hand.

Lucinda returned her hands to her lap and tilted her head slightly.

"Miss Archer doesn't live in the same house, does she?"

"She does," I said. "Why do you ask?"

"Oh." She straightened her back a bit. "You two are…friends? She seemed a bit cold and unfriendly just now."

"She's not unfriendly," I snapped.

Lucinda dropped her eyes to the table.

"Apologies. I'm being a git." I released a long exhale. "Things are a bit complicated between Nora and I."

She raised her gaze. "You have feelings for her though, don't you?"

I swallowed again. "Yes. Very much so, actually."

She gave a stiff nod and studied the perspiration on her water glass. "I must ask then…if you have feelings for this Miss Archer woman, why did you and Elsie set up this lunch date then?"

My eyebrows went up. "Pardon?"

"You and your sister," she said. "The two of you were to meet for lunch and then she would pretend she had an appointment so you and I could…" Her shoulders lowered. "You weren't involved in the scheme at all, were you?"

I winced. "I'm going to kill my sister for this, if that helps at all."

Lucinda's mouth puckered and twisted as she struggled to maintain her composure. "I think I will go." She slowly rose from her chair and slid her bag over her arm. "I don't especially like being made a fool of, you understand."

I didn't blame her. In fact, part of me wanted to flee too.

"I understand. I am so sorry Elsie put you in this situation." I shook my head. "At least stay for a cup of tea."

"No, I don't think I will stay." She gave another stiff nod. "Good afternoon, Jack." She turned on her heel and disappeared around the corner.

I slumped down in my chair as two meals were brought out to the table and placed in front of me. The couple at the next table snickered, and I looked over at them just in time to catch them quickly turning away.

I glowered at them. "Enjoying the spectacle, are we?"

It was late in the afternoon when I returned to the Sampson

home, a wicker basket under my arm and a brown paper bag in my other hand.

Mr. Sampson was in his favourite chair in the living room, smoking his pipe and reading the newspaper. He nodded to me as I came in and passed through to the kitchen. Mrs. Sampson was busy preparing something for dinner and the combination of rich flavors in the air made my stomach grumble. I had only eaten a little of my lunch, alone at the café, and requested restaurant staff put Lucinda's lunch in a bag so I could take it home with me. No need to waste perfectly good food. There was a war on, after all.

"How was the zoo?"

"We just got back," Mrs. Sampson said, stirring something in a bowl. "A lot of their more exciting animals aren't even there right now because of the raids, but Marvin still loves it all the same."

"I can believe it."

"Did you have a nice lunch?" Mrs. Sampson smiled sweetly at me. "Your girlfriend?"

"No. No, no, no. Nothing like that." I set the paper bag on the counter. "She actually ended up leaving early so I took her meal home. Thought you might be able to make use of a salad with dinner."

She hmmed and peered inside the bag. "I'm sure I can manage something."

With a nod I headed upstairs. Nora's bedroom was empty but I found Marvin in his room, stretched out on his bed and reading a book on marsupials. Multiple posters of exotic animals decorated the walls, Sellotaped to sky blue walls. Two shelves jammed with books and toys flanked his open window, its blue gingham curtain softly billowing in the warm breeze. I gave his doorframe a little knock and he looked up from his reading.

I eyed his book and frowned. "Shouldn't you be studying for finals?"

He wrinkled his nose. "I'm studying later, I swear."

"I'm joking. Did you have fun at the zoo?"

He nodded, his whole face glowing.

I frowned. "I just wanted to let you know that I didn't have any luck finding that book you wanted. I tried several bookstores but none of them carried it."

He shrugged. "It's okay."

"However, I thought of something that might make up for it." I carefully placed the basket on the end of his bed and stepped back again, crossing my arms and leaning in the doorway.

Marvin lifted the wicker flap on the basket and let out a little shriek. He slapped his hands over his mouth, his eyes shiny with tears.

Marvin very carefully scooped the sleepy Beagle puppy out of the basket. Her copper ears were long and floppy and her dark eyes wandered around the room as Marvin cradled her to his chest.

"You got me a puppy?" Marvin squeaked. "Do Mum and Dad know?"

"Not yet."

The puppy stretched to sniff Marvin's chin, giving it a little lick with her pink tongue. He giggled and gazed down at the puppy in his arms with just as much affection as I thought he would.

"You have to promise to walk her before school, after school, and then again after dinner. You have to feed her and make sure she always has water," I said. "A puppy is a big responsibility."

Marvin was barely listening to me, still gazing adoringly at his new companion. "Uh huh."

"You'll have to come up with a name for her," I added.

Marvin and I heard footsteps on the stairs and we could tell from the weight and speed that it was Nora.

Marvin called, "Nora, come here."

Nora threw me a cold glance before poking her head around the doorframe. She was so close to me and yet felt so far away. I uncrossed my arms and moved aside so not to crowd her. I had no desire to be in her space when I was not wanted.

Nora's eyes went large when she spotted the puppy. "Oh, my goodness!" She rushed in and sat on the edge of Marvin's bed. "Hello, sweetheart."

"Jack got her for me," Marvin said, beaming.

Nora's eyebrows shot up. "Did he?" She looked at me. "Did you ask Harry and Gloria?"

I shook my head and Nora's mouth tightened. "Oh, boy."

She pet its head with the tips of two fingers, ever so gently, and rubbed behind its velvety ears.

"Aren't you just a darling?" Nora cooed. "Does she have a name?"

"What do you think of the name Ginger?" Marvin looked up at Nora with round, hopeful eyes.

"I think that's a perfect name," she said, "especially with those fabulous ears." Nora stood up and left the room, murmuring, "Can I talk to you upstairs?" on her way by.

I followed her up to the garret and swallowed as she placed her hands on her waist and stared at me.

"Have you gone completely mad?" she hissed.

"The boy is old enough to have a puppy. I got a puppy at that age and it was fine."

"It's not up to you, Jack," she said. "I can't *believe* you didn't ask Gloria. What if she says he can't keep it? What then?"

"She won't—"

"Oh, really? You know that for certain?" She closed her eyes and shook her head. "You're risking breaking that boy's heart because you think you know how my aunt will react? Because you know her so well?"

"Your uncle won't care," I added for good measure.

She rolled her eyes. "The house could get bombed and Harry would simply keep on reading his newspaper. But Gloria isn't like that. Do you think there's a chance Marvin hasn't been asking them for a puppy for *years*? If they wanted him to have one, they would have given him one."

"I'm not going to apologize for doing something nice for the kid." I crossed my arms over my chest. "Perhaps we should stop pretending me getting a puppy for Marvin is what you're *actually* angry about."

Nora slowly turned to look at me. "Oh, I can be angry about more than one thing at a time, I promise you that."

"Elsie set it up," I said. "She asked me to go to lunch with her, Lucinda showed up, and then Elsie left, saying something about an appointment she forgot about. Lucinda thought I was in on the charade and left a few minutes after you saw us together. It was *nothing*."

"Why would your sister do that? She knows we're..." she struggled to find the right word and finally flicked her hand dismissively, "whatever we are. She *must* know there is something going on between us."

"I have no idea, but when I see her next I am going to set things straight and tell her you and I are together." I lowered my voice slightly. "I'll tell her I love you."

Nora eyes went from fiery fury to dull weariness, and she was silent for a moment. "If we're supposed to be together and in love, why can't I trust you fully?"

My mouth fell open slightly. I wasn't sure if she was asking me or if the question was rhetorical. Either way, our conversation was interrupted by the sound of Mrs. Sampson's voice downstairs.

"My lord! Where did that come from?"

Nora closed her eyes tight. "Here we go."

seventeen

Nora

Uncle Harry peered around the edge of his newspaper and frowned at the adorable Beagle puppy under Marvin's arm, smelling the air frantically as her new best friend crunched on his toast.

"Must Ginger join us for breakfast?" Harry grumbled, reaching for his tea.

"Yes, dear. Ginger is to stay on the floor during meals," Gloria added. "Did you walk her this morning?"

Marvin carefully set the puppy down by his feet. "I did."

Ginger, unbothered by her eviction, sniffed around the table legs hunting for crumbs.

Gloria, as I expected, was gobsmacked Jack gave Marvin a puppy without speaking to her first and seemed very ready to tell him to take the puppy back straight away. But when Marvin foisted the puppy into her arms and Ginger looked up at her with her big chocolate eyes, Gloria blinked down at her.

"Goodness," she'd said. "Her ears are far too long for the rest of her body."

Ginger had simply rested her little head on Gloria's shoulder and fallen asleep. Gloria's determination crumbled in an instant. And just like that, Ginger was a part of the Sampson home and Jack was Marvin's hero—even more than he was already.

"I told you it would be fine," he whispered to me later that evening. "You got lucky."

I quickly fell in love with Ginger like the rest of the family, but I still didn't like the way he undermined my aunt and uncle and thought it was fine. It was *their* house and it was *their* son. It was a step too far.

I went to bed early that night and then spent Sunday at the shop, catching up on some projects and, yes, avoiding Jack.

Jack and Lucinda looked like they fit together so well when I spotted them at the café. They knew the same people, the same culture, the same world. Meanwhile, I was only the hired help.

On Sunday night, I found a letter on my pillow.

I hope you're not avoiding me. You must know there really is nothing between Lucinda and I. I'm seeing my sister in a few days and I'm going to get to the bottom of this. I understand WD hurt you and made it hard for you to trust again. I swear you're the only one I want. Whenever you're ready to talk about it, you know where to find me. -J

At least he knew well enough to give me some space to consider why I felt so conflicted about him.

As I walked from my bus stop in Camden to Cider Lane on Monday morning, I thought about the promises I made to myself after Warren Denning nearly ruined my life. I vowed I would never lose my head over a man ever again and I specifically swore off men from affluent families.

And now I'd gone and done both.

But Jack was right; in my heart, I knew there was nothing going on between him and Lucinda. But that gnawing uncertainty *was* a problem. My insecurities were not his fault *or* his doing. I was being a jealous fool for no good reason and it was hurting both of us.

I just wasn't sure how to get over it.

It began to rain as I stuck my key in the lock of my shop door.

"Good morning, Miss Archer," Mr. Culpepper said from the doorway of the nearby cobbler shop. "Were you able to find any paint for the outside of the top? 'T'would make it a might nicer looking, I reckon."

"Good morning, Mr. Culpepper," I said, realizing my key was stuck in the lock. I wiggled it and wrenched on it but the key would not turn. "I bought the paint but I haven't had the time to paint it."

"My son could paint it for you, miss. He charges a reasonable price and not a penny more." He paused. "He's not married, either, I might add. Handsome like his pa too."

I smiled at him over my shoulder. "Is that so?"

"Aye, miss." He winked. "Should I tell him to drop by your shop sometime with his brushes?"

"Sure. It needs to be done I suppose. Thank you." I nodded and he disappeared back into his shop.

I turned back to the shop door, glared at it, and gave it a good thump with my fist—a trick I'd tried many times before. That day it actually worked—the key fell limply out of the lock and onto my shoe. I let myself in and began the business of the day.

A chap who paints buildings for a living, I thought, with a papa who fixes shoes. That was the kind of simple, uncomplicated, straightforward man I should be with. Not someone like Jack. Jack considered himself an academic, unattached to the privilege of his youth, and unaffected by his family's excess of advantages. He pretended he was above that but that's not something you can simply walk away from. It was as much a part of him as my own upbringing was a part of me. It was the foundation of our lives. To believe that gulf wouldn't cause problems in a relationship was incredibly naïve.

I was lost in thought when a well-dressed young woman entered the shop, a dripping umbrella under her arm.

"Good morning," she said, pulling a small packet out of her bag. "Do you think you could repair these?"

She carefully placed a pair of delicate white gloves on the counter. A cluster of pink and yellow flowers was embroidered on each near the wrist. Each glove had a few small rips along the seams of a couple fingers—four rips on the left hand and two on the right.

"You must be left handed. I usually see more tears like this on the right glove," I said. "Yes, I can certainly fix these for you."

She beamed. "Excellent."

I explained when I could have them back to her, the cost for fixing them, my usual spiel. As I studied the tears again and the customer turned to leave, my mind went back to that day I sat in Mrs. Foster-Quinn's parlour as she and Mrs. Pope discussed Lucinda and Jack's wedding. Mrs. Pope had gloves like these slung over her purse. They were the gloves of someone from the same city and, at the same time, an entirely different planet.

The woman turned back to me, hesitating. "A friend of mine told me you have some off-ration stockings for sale."

I wondered who her friend was. Mrs. Garnier? Elsie? Someone else within their circle perhaps? A pang of hate towards Elsie nearly made me wince.

She pretended to be my friend, and then set Jack up on a lunch date with someone else? Why would she do that?

I grabbed a few cardboard sleeves from under the counter and spread them out flat next to her gloves. "They're quite nice. How many pairs would you like?"

The woman inspected them and picked one up. "These *are* quite nice. I'll just take the one for now."

She paid me and left, opening her umbrella as she ducked out into the rain. It was coming down harder now, streaming off the roof and collecting on the pavement.

I went to work fiddling with a half-finished garment on a dress form when the front door opened again. This time it was a middle-aged man in a black coat and a dark grey fedora. His mouth was a hard line and his eyes narrowed as they landed on me.

Men rarely came into my shop—and never men who looked as serious as this chap.

"Good morning," I said, fighting the quaver in my voice and moving behind the counter. "How can I help you?"

"Are you Miss Nora Archer?"

I swallowed. "Yes?"

"I'm Stewart Milton and I work for the Board of Trade. My department was recently notified that you are in possession of silk stockings, and you have been selling them from this shop without the use of ration coupons." His dull grey eyes locked with mine and his monotone timbre droned. "Is this accurate?"

I quickly realized the customer from that morning wasn't a real customer at all. But it couldn't have been *just* her who tipped off the government. Someone else must have talked to get them to send someone in.

My chest tightened. "I…I don't know what you're referring to."

Mr. Milton tipped his head. "I think you know exactly what I'm talking about, Miss Archer." He stepped closer to the counter. "It's a very nice shop. Please don't make me tear it apart to find them. It'll be easier for both of us if you just show me where the black-market stockings are."

"I need to see some identification," I said, barely above a whisper. "How do I know you even work for the government?"

He sighed, annoyed, and handed his ID card to me. With a shaky hand I gave it back to him.

Biting the inside of my lip and staring at him, my chest heaved. I decided to do the only thing I *could* do.

Closing my eyes, I released a long, unsteady breath. I dragged the carton from under the counter and slid it towards him, my eyes lowered.

He removed the cover and slid the stockings out of the box, inspecting them closely. "I see."

This is very, very bad.

"The previous owner left them here," I blurted. "I moved into this shop a few months ago and they were in a box in the back room when I moved in."

"Indeed," he mumbled, sliding them back into the box without looking up at me. "Miss Archer, I am going to ask you to come with me. I trust you realize how serious this is."

"Am I under arrest?"

"I'm not a police officer," he said. "But I expect criminal charges will be laid against you, yes."

My vision clouded with tears. What happened next was a bit of a blur, but I was suddenly in the back of his car, the box of stockings in the boot. He navigated through the soaked London streets, heading to Westminster.

Once I regained a bit of control over my breathing, I forced myself to focus on what questions they would ask me and what I could say. The most important thing to me was to protect Irene, no matter what that meant for me.

I only wished I could get a message to Irene and her brother to take care and stay away from the shop.

Keeping my head down as we walked, I was hustled down a bleak, sterile hallway. Two women whispered to one another as they saw us, and I definitely heard one of them mutter "stockings" as we went by. Mr. Milton showed me to a small office and told me to take a seat. He hung his coat and took a seat behind his desk, lighting a cigarette and exhaling the smoke out of his nostrils as he studied me. He plucked a pen from his desk and prepared to write on a fresh piece of blank paper.

"Where did you get the stockings, Miss Archer?"

"I told you. They were there in the back room when I moved into the shop a few months ago. The former owner must have left them there."

"Why not sell them legitimately?"

"I'm a service-based business," I said, straightening my shoulders. "I didn't want to go through the hassle of registering to sell products and take ration coupons for them, not for a few silly stockings."

Mr. Milton lowered his chin, looking at me with a cold expression. "But they're not just silly stockings, are they? They are extremely rare and valuable goods at the moment."

I shrugged. "I suppose."

"So, you couldn't be bothered to register for the coupon scheme," he confirmed, jotting notes. "Why not sell them to another business then? Why choose to sell them yourself?"

"I knew I could make more money selling them separately."

I also knew selling a lot of stockings to one shop could potentially tie us back to Eddie's dockyard theft. Selling them separately was safer—but Mr. Milton didn't need to know that bit.

"How many pairs did you sell?"

"Four or five."

That wasn't true either.

"To how many different people?"

"Two."

Also a lie.

"What are the names of the people who purchased the four or five pairs of stockings from you?"

"I don't know their names."

Another lie. And Mr. Milton knew it.

"Were they all clients of yours you did sewing work for?" His eyes narrowed again.

"No."

"How many *were* clients?"

"None of them."

Mr. Milton tossed his pen down and pinched the bridge of his nose. "Miss Archer, let me be very clear. I've been tasked with getting names of your customers and finding out where you actually got those stockings."

"I'm sorry," I said, finally able to meet his gaze. "I would love to help you, but unfortunately I can't."

"If I look in your business transaction log I'm not going to see anything about stockings, am I?"

"Mending, yes. Selling, no."

He sat back in his chair and glared at me. "You're a young woman with a new business, you seem very bright and capable. What I don't understand is why you would risk getting into legal trouble to make a few extra pounds from some stockings. It doesn't add up."

"You just said it yourself—I had a new business," I said. "There are so many expenses that go into a new business, you know. Renting a commercial space, making repairs, buying supplies."

"I understand—"

"Fabric is more expensive than before the war but I'm sure you know about that—"

"I'm aware—"

"Advertising, utilities, signage—"

"You've made your point, Miss Archer."

Folding my hands neatly in my lap, I smiled at him.

"You ought not to look so smug, Miss Archer," he said quietly. "I'm giving you a fine."

My smile disappeared and my stomach twisted.

"A fine? I have nothing else to sell. You can't just let me off with a warning?"

His glower deepened, his nostrils flaring like mad. "No. You're lucky you're not seeing the inside of a jail cell."

I sat back in my chair, as if I could sit back so far that I might just disappear completely into it. No such luck.

"We're giving you a fine of seventy-five pounds, and you have two weeks to pay it."

A breath forced its way from my lips. "Seventy-five quid? How on earth am I supposed to get seventy-five quid in two weeks?"

"That is not my concern," he clarified. "Perhaps you should have avoided breaking the law. These laws are in place for important reasons. There's a war on. We all have to make sacrifices."

"I'm aware there is a war on, Mr. Milton."

"Good." He inhaled deeply from his cigarette and set it down in the ashtray again. "However, since you're not likely to commit this type of crime again, like you said, I am willing to negotiate."

"Negotiate?"

"I am willing to void the fine if you tell me the names of both people you sold stockings to *or* you tell me where you *actually* got the stockings. We'll take either one."

It could have been so simple. I could have opened my mouth and let the names of the affluent women just tumble from my lips. It would have been so easy and it would have solved everything. Those customers would have been tracked down and fined, yes, but they could probably handle the financial strain—unlike myself.

I looked at him right in the eye. "I'll tell you their names of my customers."

He picked up his pen.

"Princess Margaret and Clementine Churchill." I leaned forward in my chair. "You're not writing that down?"

eighteen

JACK

"I hope you're ready to explain why you did what you did."

I crossed my arms over my chest from Elsie's bedroom doorway on Tuesday evening, glaring at her as she read *Mansfield Park* from the comfort of her luxurious canopy bed.

She flicked to the next page. "I don't know what you mean."

"Elsie, stop being a child. This isn't a game," I snapped. "Nora saw us together at the café and now she thinks there is something between Lucinda and I."

She glanced up at me. "There has *always* been something between the two of you though."

"No," I said firmly. "There hasn't."

"She has certainly pined for you for years. She's quite a catch."

"I'm sure she will make a picture-perfect wife for someone, but that person is not me. You can't just force me to have feelings for her." I threw her a smug sneer. "It'd be like if you tried to make Percy have feelings for you."

Elsie's eyes blazed. "It is certainly *not* the same."

My remark was perhaps a bit harsh, considering the torch she carried for Percy for their entire adolescence, only to find out he fancied men.

"Nora has barely spoken to me since," I added. "Do you really want me to be with Lucinda or do you simply dislike Nora that much?"

My sister folded her hands in her lap as she thought about her reply. "I don't have anything against Nora. She seems very ambitious and talented. Lucinda just fits in so well with us."

I narrowed my eyes. "That's part of the problem."

"Oh, yes. Sure." She deepened her voice slightly. "I'm Jack Parker and I'm a man of the people. I'm basically a commoner, really, if you don't count the Cambridge education and the equestrian lessons as a child and the fencing lessons and the hunting trips with my stepfather and brother—"

"I never *liked* the hunting trips. You know that."

"Yes, they must have been quite trying for you, I imagine—"

"I live in a garret and make a teacher's salary," I said flatly. "I'm hardly living a life of luxury."

Mum emerged from her sitting room down the hall, clutching a newspaper in her hand. "Can you two please stop bickering? It's giving me a headache."

"Sorry, Mum," I mumbled.

"I'm glad you're here," she said, far too casually. "I wanted to ask you for details on Nora's arrest."

I widened my eyes. "Pardon?"

Mum blinked at me. "Nora Archer, your…friend. She was arrested yesterday."

Laughing, I shook my head. "You're mad. What are you on about?"

"Archer Fashion & Tailoring." she said, thumbing through the pages of the newspaper in her hand. "That's her shop, isn't it? I assumed you already knew about it." She folded the paper over and handed it to me so I could read the small black and white print.

Elsie tossed her book aside and practically leapt from her bed to read over my shoulder. "Really? What did she do?"

There it was, in a small square with a bold headline: *Seamstress arrested for stockings racket.* Details were scant but it certainly sounded like the same Nora Archer—seamstress in Camden, owner of Archer Fashion & Tailoring.

"This has to be a mistake," I said.

I thought back to the past meals I'd shared with the Sampsons. They would certainly know about Nora's arrest. If she hadn't told them herself, Mr. Sampson would certainly have seen it in the newspaper as Mum had. Nora was absent from dinner the night before and breakfast was nearly silent that morning. Now I knew why.

Why didn't she tell me?

As I lowered the newspaper, Mum carefully slid it from my hand.

"This is truly devastating news," she said. "Oh, no. That is dreadful."

I raised my eyebrows at her, shocked at her response. And then I realized why.

"We had a criminal in our *home*. What will people think?" She let out a heavy sigh. "People will think we dine and entertain with murderers and thieves, that's what they'll think." Mum put a hand to her forehead. "This is a disaster."

"It must be a misunderstanding," I said. "I'll talk to her about it tonight. Nora isn't that type of person."

My mother slowly lowered her hand and frowned, the faint lines around her eyes deepening. "Darling, you're not *with* that girl, are you?"

"Why is that so hard for the two of you to believe? She's smart and funny and beautiful and—"

"Of course she is, sweetheart," she said. "But she's also a felon. I've read delinquents can be quite charming."

I threw my hands up in the air. "I'm not going to stand here and listen to you talk about the woman I love—"

"Love?" Elsie repeated.

If I didn't know better, I would say a glimmer of regret crossed her face. Mum was less concerned.

"Darling, you only *think* you love her. But you don't. Not really. Do you even really *know* this girl?" Sliding her arm under mine, Mum gave me a knowing smile. "Because I know *my* boy, my angel, would not knowingly be with someone who would get involved in some illegal scheme with black-market stockings."

Elsie lowered her eyes.

A storm of conflicting emotions swirled in my head. It didn't make any sense.

"I'm going home," I said, turning and heading for the door.

"Jack, you need to end things with her."

I slowly turned to face my mother again. "No."

"You know your father wants to run as an MP once Archie gets back and takes over the business," she said.

If *he comes back.*

"And?"

"Reporters love this sort of thing. They love digging into the personal lives of politicians and finding stories exactly like this." She held up the newspaper. "Something like this could end his career before it's even started."

"If a small misunderstanding like this could end his political career so quickly, perhaps he does not have the stomach for a career in Parliament."

"Jack, this is not a game. You need to end things with her before things go any further."

"I can't," I said.

"You can and you must," she said. "She has put us all at risk. We had her in our home. We hired her. You are...romantically involved with her. It cannot go any further, Jack. You have to understand how damaging this is to all of us. If you won't think of your father's career, at least consider your own. Do you think Cambridge will want you back when they find out about you and a criminal?"

In my bones and in my blood, I knew I would likely love her no matter what she did. She could burn Harrods down and I would probably crawl back to her on my hands and knees. But the last few days had been confusing—she couldn't bring herself to trust me even though I didn't betray her. Was fighting for someone who didn't trust me worth it if she could hurt my family? I wasn't so sure.

"I'll clear things up with her when I get home," I said quietly, my eyes landing on the floor. "There must be more to it than that."

I wanted to grab that newspaper, hold it over an open flame, then scour all of London for the other copies and burn them as well.

"Will you please stay for dinner?" Elsie asked, her voice softer than usual.

I pinched the bridge of my nose. It seemed like Mum's headache was catching. "Fine."

"Lovely," Mum said, sweeping down the hall. "By the way, Lucinda Pope is coming to dinner too and I have the two of you seated together. I know how well you two get on."

My jaw tightened so severely my teeth ached.

Before I could reply, Mum spoke again. "Oh, before I forget—your father wants to talk to you. He's in his office."

I stalked out of the room, my nostrils flaring as I made my way through the grand house. Before I knocked on the intricately carved wooden door with the golden brass handle, I took a few deep breaths to steady myself.

I rapped on the door and my stepfather gave a low, "Yes?"

Letting myself in, I closed the door behind me and clasped my hands together behind my back as if I was awaiting orders from my general. "Mother said you wished to speak to me."

He nodded at me and gestured to the chair in front of his desk, all without a hint of eye contact. As I took a seat he tented his fingers, his gaze still resting on the papers on his desk.

"We should talk about your future," he said.

The words sent ice through my veins. "Surely not yet."

"You have a lot to catch up on."

"Archie could still come back," I said. "He could still—"

"You don't know that." He finally raised his eyes to me. "None of us know what is going to happen. We need to prepare..." He cleared his throat. "We need to prepare for the worst."

I straightened. "I'm already on contract to teach at Highgate Grammar again next year."

That wasn't entirely true. I expected to be offered a second contract soon but no papers were *technically* signed yet.

"Then I suggest you let them know you will be breaking your contract," my father replied coolly. "You're needed elsewhere. The manufacturing of uniforms takes priority over teaching at the moment. We all have to make sacrifices."

"But I'm only teaching because that's where I was placed for official war duties. They probably wouldn't let me go even if I wanted—"

"I've already spoken to someone at the War Office about your duties. It's taken care of."

My chest tightened. "But I don't know anything about the business. I would be more of a hindrance than a help. You must have someone else—"

"Someone else I could trust more than my own stepson? Of course not," he snapped.

Even now, he couldn't bring himself to call me his son. I would always be the spare to him.

"I know you would be coming into the industry blind," he continued, stoic once more. "That's why I want you to begin your duties in August when the term is over. We can't waste any more time."

I paused, my head swimming. "What about when the war is over and things slow down again?"

He picked up a pen and lifted one of the papers from his desk. "You would need to continue. I can't waste time educating you on the business for you to scurry back to Cambridge when it's convenient for you."

My stomach turned. Scurry. Like I was a mischievous rodent he needed to deal with.

"Do you understand?" He lifted an eyebrow slightly.

I gave a slow nod. "Yes."

He reached for his telephone—my cue to leave his office. I wanted to run out of there screaming, slamming the door behind me. Instead I stiffly walked out, shutting the door gently behind me, like the obedient little son I was trained to be.

nineteen

Nora

⸎

Things were quiet at Archer Fashion & Tailoring after the news story came out.

It wasn't even a story, really, but a puny paragraph tucked into the bottom edge of the page. And it's not like the story made it into *every* London paper. Not even close.

Just the ones my customers happened to read apparently.

I picked away at a few projects I had on the go, carefully stitching buttons down the front of a newly altered winter coat. I transformed a forgotten garment found at the back of a closet into a chic, tailored, and modern coat anyone would be proud to wear in cold weather. I was proud of it.

As I looked around my lonely shop, my stomach clenched. I had only received a handful of new projects to work on since the news of my extensive criminal network broke out.

When I arrived at the shop that morning, Mr. Culpepper shook his head at me and slammed his door shut.

At least he'll stop asking me about getting the front of the shop painted, so not a total loss there.

I kept reminding myself Irene was safe. Her brother was safe. That's what was most important.

Mr. Milton took me in his motorcar to Scotland Yard where I was officially written up for profiteering and given my fine. I was in a stunned daze as a young clerk rolled my inked fingerprints across a piece of card and then ordered me to stand by a wall so she could take my photograph.

I blinked at her, clenching my hands to stop them from shaking. "My photograph?"

I thought back to my scandalous photography business with Maisie and the memory of it brought me a glimmer of comfort in that darkest of moments.

The clerk lowered her voice and frowned. "Your mug shot."

My breath caught in my throat as I gaped at her.

"Oh. Yes. Right." I swallowed and stood as directed and turning when told as tears pricked the back of my eyes.

As I took the tube home after my release, I thought of Irene. I needed to get a message to Irene—I needed her to stay away from the shop in case the government had eyes on me. I couldn't be sure they hadn't nabbed Irene too for that matter. I couldn't even drop by her flat in case I was followed.

Then there was the matter of the fine to consider.

I would have to give up the shop and sell everything, there was nothing else for it. I would have to go back to Scotland Yard—or maybe Mr. Milton could?—and beg and grovel for some kind of payment plan. I would have to go back to working in someone else's shop. I knew that would be a whole other challenge because who on earth wants to hire a criminal to work at their shop?

I was startled from my daze when the shop door opened and Mrs. Adams came in.

I saw it straight away—the lowered eyes, the guarded expression, the unusually tight grip on her bag. The signs were all there. Everyone in the entire bloody city had seen my name in print it seemed.

"Good afternoon," I said brightly. "You must be here for those trousers. I'll just go grab those for you."

She nodded stiffly, still not meeting my gaze.

"Here you are," I said, sliding two pairs of adjusted, pressed, and neatly folded trousers on the counter before tucking them into a bag for her and telling her the fee.

Mrs. Adams tossed the money on the counter and snatched the bag, turning around. She stopped and faced me again, wincing.

"Yes? Is there something else I can help you with?" My voice was nearly pleading. I hated it.

She shook her head, her face pinched with puzzlement. "You seem like such a nice girl. I can't understand it."

I wanted to shout, "It was for a friend!" but couldn't, of course.

"They didn't get *all* the details in that story," I said, my tone more timid than usual.

She gave me a curt nod and left without another word.

My shoulders fell as I let out an exasperated sigh. That was the sixth customer I'd had in the two days since the story was printed who basically displayed the same reaction—they were disappointed in me and confused why a "nice girl" like me would break the law. I doubted I would see any of them ever again.

I found a sheet of paper, tore it in half, and wrote a note to Irene on it. I'd have to mail the bloody thing to her if I didn't figure out a better solution. I stuck it in an envelope, wrote her address on it, and stuffed it in my bag.

It was nearly five o'clock when I closed up shop for the day. As I started for the nearby bus stop, I was surprised to see Jack's tall frame approaching me. We silently met in the middle space between us, not saying a word for a moment. It was only a few days since we spoke, but it felt like months. I looked up at him and studied the soft green of his eyes, his waves of blond hair, and the gentle curves of his lips—I felt like I knew it all so well. However, he had shadows under his eyes, and there was a coolness in his gaze.

I wanted nothing more than to wrap my arms around his neck and kiss that mouth until I couldn't feel the ruin any more. I wanted to replace my self-loathing, if only for a little while, with the sensation of his skin against mine.

"Hello," I said.

"Hello." With his hands in his trouser pockets, he gave a little sideways nod. "Let's go to the park and have a chat."

I nodded and slipped my hand under his arm as we made our way to St. Martin's Gardens only a quick walk from my shop. We slid onto a bench and I tucked one leg under myself. I craved the feeling of the grass on my feet but I wasn't about to get grass stains on one of my precious pairs of stockings—especially now that I didn't have a ready supply of them on hand.

Sitting sideways and watching him carefully, I could tell something was wrong. He couldn't maintain eye contact with me, and he hadn't smiled once. I could have sworn he flinched when I took his arm.

He knows.

"I take it you're not upset with me anymore over that silly business with Lucinda," he said, barely glancing my way.

I shook my head. "I shouldn't have taken my insecurities out on you. I'm so sorry." I shrugged. "I'm a jealous fool."

The corner of his mouth curved into a tiny smile that didn't reach his eyes.

"I take it you saw my name in the paper," I said.

There was no use hiding from it. He either knew about it already or needed to be told.

Jack stared straight ahead. "Yes. I saw it."

"A friend gave them to me and with the shop just starting up, I thought I could make a few extra pounds from them. It was stupid and I wish I hadn't done it, but it seemed like a harmless, temporary thing." I lowered my eyes. "And then I got caught."

He gave a little nod. "I really wish you hadn't taken them." He looked at me. "If you wanted money for your friend, you could have asked me."

"You hate taking money from your family."

"I would have done if it would have kept you out of trouble," he said, his jaw tightening. "My mum practically threw the newspaper in my face."

I winced. "They know too. Lovely."

"I should have learned about it from you, Nora, not them. I felt like a bloody fool."

"I didn't want to get you involved. I was protecting you," I said.

He let out a long breath as his gaze hit the grass. "This whole situation has put me in a very difficult position. This could hurt my family and my career." His words sounded rehearsed.

My eyes narrowed. "Did your mother tell you to say that?"

He turned slowly, his eyes stern. "We need to end things between us."

My eyes bore into him, a combination of anger and devastation building in my stomach.

"Because I sold some stockings?" I whispered.

He jerked his gaze away when a tear rolled down my cheek.

"I'm sorry," he said flatly. "We're just too different. And you don't trust me and I don't know if I can trust someone who is…who…"

"A criminal? That's the word you're looking for, right?" I sniffed but put no effort into hiding my tears. I wanted him to see how he hurt me.

He was like a statue, his empty eyes fixed on something in the distance.

"Fine." I shook my head and fished around in my bag for a hanky. I spotted the letter tucked inside. "Do me a favor, would you?"

"What?"

I took the sealed envelope for Irene out of my bag and slid it across the bench to Jack. "Can you deliver this for me? I need someone to hand deliver it to Irene specifically. I can't do it myself because I'm afraid I'm being watched. It's very important she gets it as soon as possible."

He gave a gentle nod and subtly tucked the letter from the bench to his pocket. "I'll do it right now."

I sniffed again. "Thank you."

"Nora, I—"

"No, Jack, I don't think we have anything to say to one another after this. We should have just stayed roommates I suppose, like Gloria wanted." I gave a nod and left the bench, practically running out of the park.

I'm sure I looked a mess as I boarded a bus for Highgate, but if anyone asked I could say I lost someone in the war. A young woman crying on a bus wasn't so uncommon in those days.

But no. I was just another brokenhearted London girl in love with a man who thought he was too good for her. And maybe he was right.

twenty

JACK

———❦———

I took the tube to Deptford to find Irene Haley, all the while having no idea who she was or what might be in the envelope. When Nora asked me to deliver it for her, I would have done just about anything to bring her some comfort. I wanted to wrap my arms around her. I wanted to hold her and caress her hair. I wanted to shout how much I didn't want to end things between us—I simply had to.

I was still in a forlorn fog as I asked the chap at the tube ticket office for directions to the address on the envelope. I felt eyes linger on me as I walked, desperately searching for street signage. At the corner of Irene's street, a short and dark lane tucked off of a different short and dark lane, a young woman sat on a stoop, a baby tucked in one arm. The woman, dressed in soiled clothing, was likely not even eighteen yet.

She stretched her palm out to me. "Spare change, sir?"

My stomach in my throat, I dropped a five shillings into her hand and continued on. The Blitz was hard on everyone, but so many of the bombs dropped on the poorest regions of London, making their difficult daily lives even more of a hardship.

I wondered if Irene was a friend of Nora's. She hadn't told me anything about her. I wanted to ask but Nora left me in the park as soon as I agreed.

I found the address and rapped on the old, narrow door, much of its surface chipped away and scratched.

"Not interested in whatever 'tis you're sellin,'" said the voice of an older cockney woman from the other side of the door.

"Oh, I'm not selling anything, ma'am," I said. "Are you Irene Haley?"

"That's my daughter," she said. "Who's askin' for 'er?"

"I'm a friend of Nora Archer."

When the woman didn't reply, I wondered if I said the wrong thing. Maybe I shouldn't have given out Nora's name so freely. I took a step away from the door and slid my hand over the envelope in my pocket for the thousandth time, confirming it was still safe.

The door opened wider and a pretty blonde woman stepped out into the street. "I'm Irene. What can I do for you?"

"Irene Haley?" I repeated. "Sorry if I seem rather cloak and dagger but Nora was very specific with her instructions."

"Yes, that's me, I promise." She nodded, her eyes full of concern. "Is Nora alright?"

I retrieved the letter from my pocket and handed it to her. "She didn't tell me what the note concerned so I'd better not say."

She tore the letter open and skimmed the words on the half-page note. "Oh, god." Irene looked back up at me. "She got caught."

I gave a somber nod.

She read the note again. "Do you know how much trouble she's in?"

"I don't believe she'll imprisoned if that's what you're asking."

"You must think I'm a terrible person for putting her up to it," she said, closing her eyes. "I didn't have anyone else to ask. I thought she would be my best option." She crumpled the note in her fist.

Nora did it for her friend who needed money.

"I don't know anything about the, uh, arrangement," I said. "But I'm sure you had your reasons."

Irene Haley wasn't my favorite person in that moment, but looking around at the state of the street she lived on it was safe to assume she was desperate.

Two curious little faces peered out at me from the small window beside the door. I heard the gruff voice of a man telling them to get down from the window and they disappeared.

Irene, probably her mother, a husband or a brother, and at least two young children all lived there in that small flat.

I had to assume the inside was as dilapidated as the outside and wondered if the children or their mother were in danger living in a place like that.

"Will you see Nora again soon? Can you give her a message?"

I nodded. I couldn't see Nora wanting to talk to me again any time soon, but I would have to try.

"Please tell her I'm sorry for getting her involved and that it's all my fault." She hesitated. "Tell her…I suppose just tell her…tell her I'm sorry."

"Jack, are you alright, dear?"

My eyes shot up to see Mrs. Sampson staring back at me, a dish towel and a plate in her hand. I lowered my eyes to my full plate of food on the table in front of me.

"Sorry," I said. "I was…lost in thought." I gave my head a gentle shake, loosening the cobwebs.

"I should hope so," she said, going back to drying dishes. "You've barely touched your dinner. I thought maybe something was wrong with it."

I laughed and hid my wince as I took a gulp of room temperature tea. "Not at all. It's delicious as always. I'm just sorry I wasn't home soon enough to eat with you lot."

Ever since speaking with Irene, I kept thinking over and over how I was a fool for listening to my mum and breaking things off with Nora. Of *course* Nora had a good reason for taking such a risk. I should have known better.

"You didn't miss much," Mrs. Sampson said, reaching for another plate to dry. "It was quiet. Things are a bit difficult right now." She lowered her voice. "Did you read about Nora in the paper?"

Sticking a spoonful of potato dumplings in my mouth, I nodded.

"Poor thing." She frowned deeply and slid the dry plate into the cupboard. "She worked so hard for her shop and now she has to give it up."

I stared at her. "Why would she have to do that?"

"They gave her a fine," she whispered. "Seventy-five quid."

My shoulders fell. "I didn't know that."

"I told her she should have taken their offer so she would be done with the whole sorted business." Mrs. Sampson pursed her lips and put some flatware away.

"What offer?" I shook my head.

"They told her they would let her go no questions asked if she told them where she got the stockings or who she sold them to." She rolled her eyes. "If she's trying to be a martyr, she's doing a good job of it."

I took another sip of tea but I don't even know if it made it onto my tongue. The only thing I could taste was my own regret.

Not only had Nora chosen to have a criminal record to protect her friend and customers, she *also* had to give up her business as well.

"Do you know where Nora got the stockings in the first place?" I chewed lazily on some steamed carrots.

"Her friend Irene. She wouldn't tell me where Irene got them though. I would guess her brother had something to do with it though. He was always getting into trouble when the three of them were growing up together."

"Nora asked me to take a message to Irene this evening. That's why I was late."

"Nora made it sound like Irene's situation is pretty dire," Mrs. Sampson said, her voice still low. "She said Irene is in the family way but she's skin and bones."

I winced. "Really? I would never have guessed that woman was expecting."

"I don't know," she said with a sigh. "Maybe Nora did the right thing, protecting Irene and those customers."

"She had no reason to protect those customers. It doesn't make sense," I said. "That shop was her dream come true and now it's gone."

Just like Nora was your dream come true and now she's gone.

Mrs. Sampson scrubbed a bowl, her tone still hushed. "How bad did things *really* look for Irene?"

"I would say quite bad. Probably unsanitary." I finished off my tea. "They live in a dodgy area. I could smell, well, things I'd rather not think about while eating. I wasn't inside their home but it looked so small and there were at least four or five people living there." I shook my head and stared down at my plate, feeling my frustration from the last few weeks rising up in my chest. "She has young children living there, in *those* conditions. And why would she do that? Why would she bring her kids back when the Germans could come back any day? It makes me so bloody frustrated. I have a lot of questions for her. What kind of a person guilts a friend into selling black-market goods for them anyway? That's not a friend at all. I feel sorry for her situation but that's—"

Mrs. Sampson swallowed and spoke slowly and softly. "You're not a mother, Mr. Parker. I can't expect you to understand what it's like to send your children away."

I closed my eyes. "I didn't mean it like that—"

"No, no. I know what you meant. I understand perfectly." Her gaze looked everywhere except at me. "You don't know why Irene would be so foolish to bring her children back from the safety of the country when London could be under attack again. Believe me, we've been told we're all sorts of things—the parents who decided to bring their children home. Selfish. Half-wits. We've been told we're endangering our children. But I'm happy with the choice I made when I brought my son home. Do you think that was an easy decision to make?"

I lowered my gaze as soon as I spotted the glint of tears in her eyes.

"Of course it wasn't. My mouth ran away with me I'm afraid," I said. "I'm so sorry."

She nodded stiffly, slapped the dish towel on the counter and stormed out of the kitchen, a few plates still bobbing in the sink.

I don't think I could have ruined that day any more if I tried.

I cleared my plate, washed it, and finished drying and putting away the dishes. It was the least I could do for putting my nose precisely where it didn't belong.

As I put the last of the dishes away I tried to figure out why Nora would choose to give up her shop rather than give up the names of the people who purchased stockings from her. I understood why she would protect a long-time friend…but customers? I couldn't fathom a good possible reason for it, no matter who it was.

I wrote a short note to Nora and slipped it under her door. It only included what Irene asked me to tell her, that Irene was sorry. I wanted to tell Nora to her face. but I was too much of a coward. I already mucked up enough things in the Sampson home that evening.

Getting Mr. Sampson's recently repaired bicycle out of the garden shed, I set out to do something I was very much dreading. But I knew it had to be done.

twenty-one

Nora

—◦—

As advised, Irene stayed away from the shop and didn't try to contact me directly. This left me with a pile of socks, mittens, and scarves to darn since I couldn't pass them onto her. The small mending tasks were the only jobs keeping the lights on at Archer Fashion & Tailoring since alteration work had dried up. Not that the lights would need to be kept on for much longer.

Maybe I should go into nursing. I bet I could stitch up wounds reasonably well.

Earlier in the day I took stock of the items I could sell: my sewing machine, the desk I sat at, the chair tucked under it, the wide custom cutting counter, all the remaining fabric, my specialty sewing and measuring tools, and my dress forms. Saying goodbye to the dress forms was like saying goodbye to two chums. Seeing someone take my beautiful Singer sewing machine away would be the worst though. I wasn't sure how I would let it go without weeping.

I wondered when Gloria would want her loan paid back.

When I got home Ginger met me at the door with a string of happy barks and a wagging tail. I smiled wide, scooped her up, and held her to my chest as she wriggled to get away.

"Ginger," I said with a laugh, "why won't you let me love you?"

I relented and put her down just as I noticed Jack looking up from the armchair by the window where he was reading, his reading spectacles perched on his nose.

Why won't you let me love you?

"Hello," I said quietly.

"Hello." He gave an unsmiling nod and looked back down to his book.

Harry, reading on the couch opposite him, barely acknowledged me. But that was normal for him.

I continued on into the kitchen where Gloria was finishing dinner preparations. Ginger watched her with unparalleled focus, waiting for a scrap of something to fall to the floor.

"Do you need a hand with anything?"

"No, I'm almost done here I think." She stirred something on the hob that smelled rich. "There's a letter for you. Looked rather official." She nodded to the little basket hanging on the wall.

I thumbed through the bills until I found my mail. She was right. It *was* official. The return address was from a government office.

"Harry, Marvin, Jack," Gloria called.

I tore the letter open and skimmed the words quickly. I read it again. It wasn't possible. It didn't make sense.

My fine was paid. In full.

The letter was just a confirmation that the full amount was, in fact, paid.

I read it again.

It could have been Gloria. She was certainly generous, but it wasn't like her to pay my fine and then not tell me.

As Jack appeared in the doorway I looked up at him and blinked. He glanced down at the letter and a flicker of recognition passed over his face before quickly looking away and continuing on to the dining room.

It was Jack. It had to be. Jack paid the fine off for me.

I folded the letter and stuffed it into my brassiere. Unfortunately Harry saw and swiftly looked away.

"I'm not going to ask," he said, raising his palms as he kept walking.

I gave a nervous, half-hearted chuckle and followed him into the dining room where I ate in silence while Harry and Gloria made small talk, and Marvin slipped tiny pieces of his dinner to Ginger under the table.

After spending the entirety of the meal in silence, Jack cleared his throat.

"I just wanted you to know I've very much enjoyed living here, and I deeply appreciate you offering your home to me," he said, speaking firmly to the bowl of carrots in the middle of the table. "However, I have decided I will be moving out soon."

Gloria looked about ready to cry. "But why?"

Jack glanced at me before answering and I felt my shoulders fall.

Me. He couldn't stand to look at me any longer.

"With my brother still missing in action, I believe my presence would bring my mother some comfort so I plan to move in with my family for a while. They're in St John's Wood so I'm only a short bus ride away from school thankfully."

My uncle gave a nod. "Very well." Disinterested, he reached for the potatoes.

Frowning, Marvin's eyes went wide and he furrowed his brow, glancing at his mum for reassurance.

"I'm disappointed but I understand," Gloria said nodding slowly. "I'm sure your mother would appreciate having her son with her."

She and Jack smiled faintly at one another, and he soon excused himself from the table. Making a weak attempt at subtly, I waited a few minutes before excusing myself from the table and making my way to the garret.

Jack was on the floor, carefully packing some books into a crate, when I poked my head up from the stairwell.

"You could knock, you know," he said.

"Why are you really leaving?"

He sat up on his knees. "I just said downstairs—"

"I heard you. I was there. I want to know why you're actually leaving." I climbed the rest of the stairs and crossed my arms over my chest.

He let out a long breath. "You know why."

"Because you can't even stand the sight of me now, is that it?"

His face finally softened and his jaw unclenched. "No." He rose and dusted off his knees. "Not that."

"You obviously still care for me enough that you paid off my fine."

Jack hesitated and slowly lifted his gaze to me. "I never said I didn't care for you."

"You had to ask your parents for the money to pay it off, didn't you?"

"It doesn't matter."

"It *does* matter. It matters to me. I know it must have killed you to do that." I stepped closer to him. "Thank you for doing that. I promise I'll pay back every penny—"

"I don't want your money, Nora," Jack snapped. "I want *you.*" He walked away, yanking on a fist of hair at the back of his head. "But I can't be with you. *That's* what's killing me."

My pulse quickened so much I thought I might burst. "It was only some silly stockings. Thanks to you, it's over now. It's done. Things can go back to how they were—"

"It's not over," he said, turning around to face me. "I paid off the fine but all your customers know what you did. The fine is paid off, yes, but the damage is done. You're naive to think your business will simply magically go back to—"

"*I'm* the one who is naive about money and business? You *must* be joking."

"Why didn't you just tell the government where you got the stockings?"

"I would never turn Irene in," I exclaimed. "She's a friend and she has children—"

"What about your customers? Why not give the government *their* names instead? It would have solved everything." Jack was looking down at me, his chest heaving and standing so close I smelled the fresh aroma of his soap.

I didn't dare tell him his sister and mother were on that list.

"I couldn't," I said quietly, lowering my arms to my sides as he stepped even nearer. "They would never trust me again. Once that trust is lost…"

Our eyes met and I knew what he was thinking: I lost my trust in him over something that wasn't even real. Meanwhile, he lost trust in me over something that was very much real.

"This won't last forever," I said. "It will be forgotten about and life will carry on."

"What makes you so confident people will forget a criminal act during wartime?" He shook his head at me. "I know you care for your friend but I really wish she hadn't come to you for help—"

"The people who make it into the papers for doing things to make a little extra money are always the desperate ones who have no other option," I flared sharply. "You think anybody *wants* to take risks? You think I *wanted* to betray my country? Of course not. Meanwhile, rich bastards all over England are taking advantage of this war and making even *more* money because they happen to know the right people, and it isn't bloody fair."

Jack's shoulders straightened. "You mean rich bastards like my father?" He tipped his head. "You didn't mind his money when it was paying off your fine or paying for a night at the Savoy—"

"I didn't ask for either of those things." My throat stung as I spoke.

He narrowed his eyes at me and went back to packing things into a crate. "I don't have time for this."

I rolled my eyes and let myself out, dashing down the stairs and out of Jack Parker's life.

twenty-two

JACK

Lucinda, seated on my right, smiled serenely at me. "So, you're living with your family now?"

I picked up my glass of excessively priced wine and took an excessively generous gulp. "Correct."

It had been a week since I moved into my old bedroom in St John's Wood. Term finals were behind me, and summer holidays had just begun. So, naturally, my mother invited Lucinda to dine with the family on that Saturday evening, not needing an actual special occasion to try to force the two of us together.

Lucinda, wearing a baby pink dress and a string of pearls, seemed happy enough to pretend our recent uncomfortable lunch hadn't happened so I was content to play along as if I wasn't tremendously embarrassed about it. Meanwhile, Elsie joined in, concealing any feelings of regret for orchestrating the whole mortifying experience. It was like a game of make-believe for all—and nobody was having fun.

Lucinda winced. "You don't seem particularly happy about this development."

I glanced at her, my glass still at my lips, and snickered. "Was I being so transparent?"

"Maybe it's all the wine you're drinking, darling brother," Elsie said from my left. "Perhaps you should slow down."

I shot her a scowl. "But it's my favorite vintage, bothersome sister."

"Stop acting like a child," she hissed in a hushed voice. "You're embarrassing yourself."

"Wouldn't want that." I put my glass down and straightened my shoulders, releasing a long breath, and fighting the strength of the wine.

Lucinda and Elsie exchanged concerned glances in front of me and I rolled my eyes.

"I'm fine." My tone didn't suggest "fine," so much as "angry with the world." "I just have a bit of a headache, that's all."

Lucinda lowered her gaze, her hands folded gracefully in her lap. "I thought you might be upset about your friend, Nora."

"What about her?"

"She sold black-market stockings from her shop," she added, "and got into some trouble."

"You saw the story in the paper?"

She blinked her big, innocent eyes at me. "No, your mother told me."

My gaze slowly drifted across the tablecloth and down to where my mother sat, laughing at something one of her catty friends said.

I swallowed, feeling a hot boiling rage rising in my chest. "Lovely."

Elsie put her hand on my arm. "Don't be angry with her, Jack. It just sort of...came up in conversation."

"That doesn't seem like a realistic possibility," I said, jaw clenched. I slid my chair back abruptly and it screeched against the floor, causing many to turn to me. "Excuse me. I need some air."

From the hallway I could still hear the dull hum of their laughter, their inane chatter, their gossip, their oblivious conversations. It felt like a nail in my temple. I made my way out to the garden and sat on the bench; the same bench where I sat with Nora and told her about my upbringing.

I couldn't help but wonder how a person could change so much. I was young when Mum married my stepfather and took on the persona of Mrs. Foster-Quinn, leaving her old life behind. I still recalled her being down-to-earth before our lives changed so dramatically. I had memories of playing in the park and laughing together about the grass stains on our knees, and a leaf that had somehow gotten in her hair. I remembered her holding me tight during a fierce summer storm, and how she used to smell like baked bread from working at the bakery.

And then Robert Foster-Quinn began taking her to dinner. Suddenly she smelled of French perfume instead of fresh bread. Suddenly she stopped getting grass stains on her knees.

Had my mother put on an act to bag herself a rich man?

Had Nora? I felt guilty for having the thought but she was, technically, a criminal. I didn't know what else Nora Archer was capable of.

I rested my head in my hands, sliding my fingers through my hair.

"Jack?"

I glanced behind me to see Lucinda.

Of course she followed me out here. I can't be alone for two bloody minutes.

"Sorry," I mumbled just loud enough for her to hear. "I'm fine. Just feeling a bit off tonight."

She silently joined me on the bench, her eyes fixed on the fountain in front of us.

"Travel," she finally said.

"Pardon?"

"At our fake lunch date, you asked me what I do for fun." She glanced up at me, a small smile playing on her lips. It was almost a self-satisfied smile, certainly not one I'd seen her use before. "I like to travel."

"What else?"

She considered. "Equestrian. In my younger days, I racked up quite a few ribbons and trophies for show jumping." She let out a long breath and went back to staring at the fountain. "And I like writing."

"Fiction? Poetry?"

"No," she said, nearly scoffing while pulling a slim, glossy cigarette case from her pocket. "Travel writing. I want to write travel memoirs." She raised an eyebrow to me, offering me one.

I laughed as I looked at her. "Who *are* you?"

She let out a small, quiet chuckle and lit a cigarette, blowing the smoke from the corner of her lips. "Traveling to all the most fascinating parts of the world and writing about them isn't quite what my parents want for me though."

"What *do* they want for you?"

"They want me to try to make Robert Foster-Quinn's stepson fall in love with me."

I winced.

She looked up at me and rolled her eyes. "It's quite clear that is never going to happen though, since he is obviously in love with someone else."

"I'm sorry if I ever gave you any indication that I—"

"You never did. Truly," she said. "And yet my father insisted I keep trying, and my mother demanded I use the methods she ensnared my father with." She closed her eyes. "I've spent years of my life humiliating myself. It's got to end." She opened her eyes again and looked right at me. "What makes the whole thing even more absurd is that I have *never* fancied you."

I burst out laughing. "Never? Really?"

"No!" She laughed and it sounded so real, unlike the smothered little chirp she usually made. "Sorry, but no."

I snorted with laughter. "I have to say, I'm a bit hurt."

"Oh, hush," she said, elbowing my arm gently.

"What about Archie? Did your parents ever suggest you try to woo *him*? He is the golden child after all."

"No. Too much competition there."

"Your parents stuck you with the bookish black sheep then? That was nice of them." I laughed again. "I'm sorry, Lucinda, for all of it. Your parents, my parents, my sister. What a mess."

We were silent a while. Finally Lucinda broke the silence again.

"No word from Archie then?"

I shook my head. "My parents have even stopped bringing up his name. Maybe they figure if they don't mention him, the fear will eventually go away."

"I assure you, it won't," she said. "My cousin is missing too."

"I'm sorry," I said. "I didn't know."

"There is a lot you don't know about me." Releasing a long, thoughtful sigh, she looked straight ahead. "To be fair, there is a lot I don't know about me either."

twenty-three

Nora

------❖------

When I returned to my bedroom after a long and dull day at the shop, I hung my bag on my doorknob and collapsed onto my bed, staring at the ceiling. I couldn't begin to guess the number of hours I spent staring at that ceiling in the dark over the few previous weeks when I should have been sleeping. The shop was failing. Irene was destitute again.

I missed working with Victoria in Covent Garden. I missed living with Maisie in Mrs. Martin's flat above the hobby shop. I missed life before the war. I missed so many things.

And then there was Jack.

I kept reminding myself some things happen and go wrong, even when they feel so very right.

The ceiling gave a little groan above me and I bolted upright. Then I heard the sound of a man's voice coming from the garret. Gloria was upstairs with him too. They sounded cordial, but I couldn't make out what they were saying. My heart leapt in my chest. and I tried to keep my breathing steady.

Jack must have changed his mind and come back!

Scrambling to my feet as I heard them coming down the creaky stairs, I waited in my doorway to greet them as Jack and Gloria arrived on the landing.

But it wasn't Jack at all.

Gloria eyed me as I blinked, confused, at the middle-aged man behind her. Stocky with a ruddy complexion, he had a high forehead, crowned with a mop of salt and pepper hair. He glanced between Gloria and I.

"Oh," I said, trying to mask the disappointment in my voice. "Hello."

He nodded at me. "Hello."

Ginger came galloping out of Marvin's room, ears flailing and tail wagging as she rushed to sniff the newcomer. Marvin chased after her, caught her, and gathered her in his arms.

"Sorry. She's very curious," he said with a laugh.

"That's alright," the man said. "I love dogs."

"Nora, Marvin, this is Mr. Hampton," Gloria said. "He's going to be renting the upstairs garret starting next week."

"Nice to meet you both," he said. "I work a lot so you probably won't see me much."

Marvin grinned at me as Ginger chewed on a chunk of his hair. "Don't go and kiss this one, too, okay?" And then he took Ginger back to his room.

My eyes went wide as I stared at the empty space where Marvin stood a moment before, a burning heat invading my neck and cheeks.

"Uh," Mr. Hampton said with an uncomfortable chuckle. "I think I'll get going. Thank you, Mrs. Sampson."

Gloria shot me a glare on her way down the stairs to show him out. I marched into Marvin's room.

"What on earth did you do that for? You were supposed to keep it a secret," I seethed.

He shrugged. "I thought you and Jack must have told Mum and that's why he moved out."

I shook my head, swinging my head hard. "No! That *isn't* what happened."

Marvin's face fell. "Oh."

A moment after the front door closed, Gloria beckoned me

downstairs. My whole body tensed up at the sound of her tone.

"I'm sorry, Nora," Marvin said, "I didn't know."

I sighed, gave a little nod, and slowly made my way to the kitchen where Gloria stood with her arms crossed and her chin the air.

"He was just joking—"

"Why would Marvin joke about you and Jack kissing out of the blue?" She arched an eyebrow at me, her lips tightly pursed. "You and Jack had a relationship, didn't you?"

I swallowed, hesitated and then gave a little nod.

"Is that why Jack ended up leaving? Because you broke his heart?"

"He broke *mine*," I snapped.

She wasn't listening. She just went on.

"I knew it," she muttered. "And that night the two of you didn't come home—you were together, weren't you?"

I lowered my eyes. "We wanted to tell you—"

"How did my boy find out? Did he walk in on the two of you in bed or something?"

"Of course not—"

Gloria's eyes became larger as she put the pieces together. "That's why Jack got him the dog, isn't it? To keep Marvin quiet."

"I told Jack that was a very *bad* idea—"

"When I wrote your mum and told her you were living with me, she warned me about taking you in." Gloria's eyes turned cold as ice as she looked at me with a mix of hatred and repulsion. "I know all about you and that married man."

"He wasn't married," I shouted before I could stop myself, "and he didn't tell me he was engaged."

She shook her head at me, her nose wrinkled. "I should have known better."

The anger bubbled over in my throat, and my eyes prickled with tears. "Is that really how you see me?"

Gloria's chest heaved. "Your mother said you were a treasure hunter but Jack Parker deserved better."

My mouth hung open as tears streamed down my cheeks.

There were no words. No words, only a hard knot of regret and heartbreak stretching from my throat to the base of my stomach.

"I think it might be time for me to leave," I whispered on my way upstairs.

"Yes, I think that would be best."

Rushing upstairs to escape the judgment in my aunt's eyes, I whipped a suitcase out from under the bed and threw it open. I grabbed four random outfits and a cardigan from my wardrobe and threw them into the case, along with some undergarments and makeup. I tossed my purse strap over my shoulder. Everything was a blur.

On my way back downstairs, I heard Marvin's voice.

"Nora, why do you have your suitcase?" He was standing in the doorway of his bedroom, Ginger squirming under one arm. "Are you leaving?"

I felt my shoulders sag. "It's alright. Everything is fine."

"Then why are you crying?"

I wiped at my eyes with the back of my hand. "It's fine, love. I just need to go."

He scrunched up his face. "Is Mum making you go?"

"No," I croaked. "It's just..." I swallowed and left him on the landing. "I'm sorry. I have to go."

I didn't look up as I made my way through the house and to the front door.

"Nora, wait," Gloria said.

"What?"

I didn't turn around. I just stood and waited for Gloria to apologize. I heard her take a step towards me.

"You'll need your ration book."

I hurled a glare at her and grabbed the little pamphlet from her outstretched hand, not making eye contact. Slamming the door behind me, I kept walking until I reached the bus stop. I sat on a nearby bench and took a few deep breaths to try to calm down while tucking my ration book into my bag.

At least Gloria didn't actively want me to starve to death—just be homeless.

As I clutched the handle on my suitcase, I realized there was only one place I could go.

I took the bus to the shop and, as always, struggled to unlock the door. But this time it was because my hands were shaking and I couldn't see through the veil of tears.

The shop was my only option. Soon, I wouldn't even have that.

twenty-four

JACK

It felt very strange walking up to the Sampson home and not just opening in the front door and letting myself in. It felt more like home to me than the house I grew up in, and yet I no longer had a key of my own.

I knocked on the door and Mrs. Sampson answered with a cautious look in her eyes and a forced smile on her lips. "Mr. Parker! How are you? Come in, come in."

I stepped inside. "I'm well. How are you?"

Before she could answer, Ginger came barrelling down the stairs and around the corner, sliding on the parquet flooring and yapping wildly. Her tailed wagged as she saw me and her barks became friendly.

I knelt to pet her. "Hello! Have you missed me, little lady? You've grown!"

Mrs. Sampson let out an irritated sigh. "I recently learned why you gave Marvin the dog."

Slowly rising again, I winced. "Oh?"

She frowned, her gaze hard. "Are you here to see Nora? Because if you are, you should know she has moved out."

"I mean, no, that's not why I'm here," I said. "We…parted ways. Where did she go?"

"No idea. We had a row and she stormed off with her suitcase." She frowned, a crease forming between her eyes.

"Oh." I swallowed and let out a breath. "Well, I owe you an apology. We shouldn't have kept our relationship from you, and we should have respected your rules while living under your roof. We never meant for Marvin to find out." I let out a long breath. "Most of all, I'm sorry I caused a strain in your relationship with your niece. I know she adores you." Wincing, I went on, "And I'm sorry for what I said about bringing children back to London. I wasn't thinking and it's absolutely none of my business. I couldn't possibly understand what any parent must go through when making that decision."

Mrs. Sampson's face softened lightly. "I appreciate you saying that, Jack." She nodded to the book under my arm. "Is that for Marvin?"

"Yes, I found it in my father's library," I said, handing over the thick reference book. "I thought Marvin would like to take a look at it. I don't expect my father has even cracked it open."

It was a book of fascinating animals found in Africa, complete with sketches and photos.

"Oh, he'll love this," Mrs. Sampson said. "Thank you."

"You can tell him he can return it whenever he's done with it." I cleared my throat. "I don't yet know if I'll be back again for another term. It's still…up in the air."

"I certainly hope so," she said. "You're his favorite teacher."

"I'm sure he's just being nice. I'm a rotten teacher."

"I don't think so. He didn't like history before, but he said you made it interesting and fun for him," she said. "That's what a good teacher does."

I smiled sheepishly. "Thank you for telling me. I appreciate that."

The weird thing was, I meant it.

Another evening at the Foster-Quinn home meant another bloody formal dinner.

"I *must* find another place to live," I grumbled to Elsie. "I can't take much more of this."

Elsie rolled her eyes at me. "Oh, stop. It's good food, small talk with family friends, and liquor."

I tugged at the collar of my shirt. "I would rather starve in silence."

Mum was practically giddy as she swanned around from guest to guest, greeting everyone, a glass of champagne in her hand.

"I didn't realize we were celebrating," I said.

"Like our mother ever needs an excuse to drink Dom Pérignon."

Mum eventually made it where Elsie and I stood off to the side.

"My darlings," she cooed. "No companions this evening?"

"Percy is off at his family's estate in the country, and Jack is still heartbroken over his femme fatale," Elsie said.

I shot her a glare. "Not funny."

"It's a shame," Mum said, barely listening, "I invited Lucinda, but her mother told me she suddenly left for Scotland a few days ago. Something about staying with friends for a few months. It's all very mysterious. Very unusual for her." She gave a little huff, spotted guests far more interesting than her children, and flew away.

When Elsie caught me smiling to myself, she raised an eyebrow at me. "What, you're proud of yourself for breaking poor Lucinda's heart? She's run off to Scotland to lick her wounds, and you're *happy* about that?"

"That's not what happened," I clarified. "She was finally honest with me. I'm hoping she left to pursue something she actually cares about."

Elsie and I took our seats in the dining room, and I felt my skin crawl as soon as I saw Warren and Helen Denning sitting directly across from us.

"Parker," he said with a nod before lazily surveying Elsie next to me. "Miss Foster-Quinn. A pleasure as always."

Elsie made a half-hearted attempt at a fake smile before turning her attention to Helen. "How are you feeling?"

Helen's hand hastily moved to her stomach. "Quite dreadful, actually. I can barely keep anything down most days."

"Get used to it, darling," Denning said, his voice entirely free of affection or empathy. "I want a big family. An entire football team of

Dennings. I expect you'll be pregnant for the next fifteen years or so."

Helen's eyes widened, and her mouth tightened at the thought.

Elsie nudged me. "Did you notice the champagne?" She pointed at the flutes placed at each table setting, already filled.

Before I could respond, my stepfather—appearing positively gleeful in comparison to his usual stoic state—tapped gently on his own champagne flute to get the attention of his guests while my mother stood at his side.

"Good evening, everyone," he said, his deep voice carrying easily throughout the room. "Before the delicious meal we have planned is brought out, we wanted to share an announcement with you, our dearest friends."

Elsie and I exchanged glances.

"Our son, Archie, is safe," Mum exclaimed, clapping her hands together, tears of joy in her eyes.

Everyone clapped, and Elsie rested her head on my shoulder, heaving a sigh of relief. "Thank God."

"We have yet to learn all the details," our father said, "but we know he escaped the POW camp while injured but managed to reach a British camp several miles away. He is now back with his own regiment and doing very well."

Mum raised her refilled champagne glass. "To Archie."

Everyone raised their flutes up and echoed her toast before downing their bubbly among cries of "Jolly good!" and "Well done, Archie!"

I felt like a weight had lifted from my shoulders. Archie was alive. I wondered how serious his injury was—perhaps he would be returning to England before the rest of his regiment. He would hate that, but our parents would certainly prefer it.

After the meal guests gathered for the usual drinks and socializing aspect of the night. As I leaned against the back wall with my perfectly aged scotch, I wondered if I could slip away to my room without anyone noticing. A few couples around my parents' age took to the dance floor, swaying to the music. One couple in particular locked eyes as they danced, like they were the only two people in the room. It was probably the thousandth time they'd shared a dance, but the way they looked at one another one might think they were falling in love for the very first time.

I thought of Nora and the dances we shared—the night we met, once in the living room, and then that night at the jazz club. I could have sworn we were supposed to grow old together and share as many dances as the couple I was watching.

Finishing off my scotch, I winced as it burned the back of my throat on its way down.

With a glass of white wine in hand Elsie joined me, tipping her head back to rest it against the wall.

"Having fun watching the old crones dance?" She gave a little laugh and sipped her wine.

"They're rather sweet, actually." I smiled, still following them from my peripheral.

Elsie studied me for a moment before her shoulders fell slightly. "Oh, no."

"What?"

"You're never going to get over her, are you?"

I scowled at her. "It hasn't even been that long."

She winced and took another gulp of wine, finishing off the glass. "You mentioned she could have her record cleared of the charges if she gave the government the list of customers who purchased black-market stockings from her."

I nodded and then glanced around to see where I might get more scotch.

"Mrs. Garnier's name would be on that list. And Mum's," Elsie said. "And mine."

As I slowly looked down at her, everything else in the room went blurry. All sounds were drowned out by the ringing in my ears.

Nora was protecting Elsie.

Nora was protecting my mother.

She didn't tell the government who bought the stockings because that would mean outing my family as traitors. That would be just as damaging to my father's reputation as me being involved with a racketeer, perhaps even more, since he also provided uniforms and textiles for the British Army.

I stared at Elsie. "Why didn't you tell me before?"

"Because I thought you would get over her. I didn't realize you actually loved her," she said. "I wanted to tell you, I swear. Mum begged me not to tell you."

My eyes landed on my mother across the room. "Tell me the truth. It was Mum who provided the tip to the authorities about Nora selling stockings, wasn't it?"

When I looked back at her, Elsie had a deep crease between her brows, and her shoulders fell. She didn't have to respond. The guilty look in her eyes said it all.

"Right," I said. "I have to get out of this house right now before I say something I will regret."

As I turned Denning popped out of nowhere like a bloody rat, grinning at me, his cheeks and nose reddened from drink. "Parker, I was wondering about your little friend Nora. Have the two of you parted ways?"

"Not now, Denning," Elsie warned.

He took a gulp from his drink. "Did she tell you we used to be chums?"

"Nora told me what you what you did to her——that you were with her and didn't tell her you were engaged. Yes, she told me." I narrowed my eyes at him. "She is an incredible woman. And you did not deserve an iota of her time." I stepped closer to him, my hands curling into fists at my sides. "You are not to breathe another word about her, do you understand me?"

"She was fun but so ignorant to think I was going to be with her when I was already engaged," he said. "It's probably good you got rid of her before your brother comes home. She would just maneuver herself into his bed next."

I grabbed the front of his shirt with my left hand and was about to wallop him with my right, but a tiny sound stopped me before I could do it.

"Warren?"

Helen stood behind Denning, her eyes wide and skin pale. I promptly let go of his shirt and dropped my hands to my sides.

"You…*dallied* with that seamstress woman while we were engaged?" she squeaked. "Did you have relations with her?"

Denning hesitated. "Uhh…"

Helen turned and fled. Denning looked back at me, set his drink down sloppily, threw his hands in the air dismissively, and went after his wife as the brown liquor seeped into the white tablecloth.

Several other guests noticed the incident and whispered among themselves. Mum sent me a curious look, and I raised my palms in response.

"I think I really would have enjoyed punching him," I said.

Elsie laughed. "Maybe one day."

After a long pause, I took Elsie's glass of wine from her and took a big gulp.

"Elsie, I'm going to get Nora back," I said. "And you're going to help me do it."

twenty-five

Nora

——◦◦◦——

If I ever thought living in my shop would be easy, I was mistaken.

I woke early to the sounds of deliveries underway on Cider Lane. I had come to despise delivery drivers, always laughing and greeting one another jovially and loudly, seemingly always right outside my shop door.

Groaning, I rubbed my sore neck and aching lower back. Throwing my blanket (two yards of Irish tweed) off and putting away my pillow (a sack of yarn), I stumbled to the WC at the rear of the shop. I began unrolling a cotton scrap tied into my hair, letting the shiny new curl fall onto my cheek before dealing with next one. I scrubbed under my arms with soap and warm water from the tiny corner sink, brushed my teeth, put on makeup, and got dressed.

This is completely fine and normal. This is temporary. I am fine.

I took myself for a morning walk to the bakery two streets away, grabbed something for breakfast, and took my usual seat on a bench in St. Martin's Gardens, specifically avoiding the bench where Jack announced he didn't want to be with me anymore.

I hated that bench. It was probably cursed or something. Stupid, hateful bench.

Despite the early morning delivery drivers on my street, Camden was mostly quiet at this time of day—still too early for most businesses to be open, and certainly too early for anyone to be in the park. So I had it to myself.

All to myself. Alone. Just me.

I chewed my scone slowly, wondering if even the woman at the bakery knew how starved I was for conversation. Probably, I guessed.

Around noon I worked on patching the elbows on an autumn coat. I was so focused on what I was doing I nearly jumped out of my skin when the door opened.

"Bloody hell," I said, clutching my chest. "Sorry, you gave me a fright—oh. Hello."

It was Gloria, who was—for some reason—dressed like she was on her way to church. She cleared her throat from her spot in front of the door.

I diligently kept at my work. "Can I help you?"

"You had someone paint your sign outside," she said quickly, her gaze hovering somewhere on the floor in front of the cutting table.

"I did it myself," I said. "I wanted some kind of proof this place did in fact exist, even if it was only for a little while."

And I had time to kill.

"It looks nice. You did a good job."

"Thank you."

Releasing a long breath after an extended pause, she came closer. "I came to say…I'm sorry." She tipped her nose up and avoided making eye contact. "I've been thinking about it, and I very much regret what I said."

I put my pins aside.

"I suppose I forgot you're not a little girl anymore," she said, her voice softening. "You must know you're the closest thing to a daughter I'll ever have. I couldn't live with myself if I didn't apologize and make sure you're okay."

I smiled, my throat stinging. "I'm sorry too. I shouldn't have lied, and I should have respected your wishes. If I could take it all back, I would."

Would I take it back? After uttering the words, I wasn't sure if I actually would or not.

Tossing the coat aside, I whipped around the counter and gave Gloria a squeeze.

"Are you alright? Where are you living anyway?"

"Here," I mumbled, "at the shop."

"Oh, Nora, sweetheart," she moaned. "No, that won't do. I'm taking you back to our house right now."

I was far too tired, sore, and lonely to object.

I nodded slowly. "Okay."

On the bus back to Highgate, Gloria leaned her shoulder against mine. "How are things between you and Mr. Parker?"

I frowned at her and simply shook my head.

"He came by the house on Saturday," she said, eyeing me as she spoke but trying far too hard to sound casual. "He brought a book for Marvin and apologized for keeping your relationship secret."

"And did you accept his apology?"

"I did."

"How did he seem?"

A few lines appeared at her eyes as she considered. "Tired. A little sad, too, I suppose, especially when he spoke of maybe not going back to teaching."

"Really? Why?" I looked up at her.

"He didn't say."

I tried to leave an appropriate pause before my follow-up.

"Did…did he ask about me?"

"He just asked where you went."

That's it?

"He paid my fine, you know," I mumbled, my gaze wandering to the window.

"He did? Really?"

I nodded. "He cares about me but doesn't want to be with me."

I wasn't looking for pity. It was just nice to have someone to talk to about that whole mess.

After a long bath and an even longer afternoon nap, I made my way downstairs around four o'clock. I could hear Gloria making dinner and I stopped when I saw a curly-haired brunette drinking tea nearby.

"Maisie!" I shrieked, throwing my arms around her and clutching her tightly.

"Hello to you too!" She slid her teacup onto the counter before my excited swaying caused her to spill.

"It's so good to see you!" I squealed. "What are you doing here?"

"I called when you were asleep to let you know I was in London, and your aunt told me to come over," she said with a laugh as I finally released her. "I'm taking you out to dinner."

I grabbed her hands and clasped them tightly. I paused and tilted my head before dropping my eyes down to her knuckles.

Sitting upon a simple shiny gold band was a glittering diamond in a square setting, flanked on both sides by triangle shoulder pieces containing diamond chips.

"Oh, my goodness," I said. "You're engaged!"

Maisie nodded vigorously, her chocolate locks bouncing. I embraced her again, somehow even tighter than before.

"I'm so happy for you!" I exclaimed into her hair.

After a few minutes of getting changed and fixing my face, we walked arm in arm to a little restaurant a few streets away, gabbing all the way.

"Tell me everything," I said. "How did Cal ask? When did he ask? Where were you when he asked?"

"It was only last week. We were having a picnic on one of my rare days off," she began.

A talented and natural photographer, Maisie was hired by the Ministry of Information to take photographs of women doing war work. She'd spent the last few months traveling all over England, taking photos of munitions factory workers, land girls, engine mechanics, drivers, members of the ATS, WRNS and the WAAF, air raid wardens—all women. Since men were needed on the front, more and more women were needed to fill those important jobs. It was a dream career for Maisie, and I was overjoyed she had found her place in the world, especially when Cal was at her side.

"We were sharing a picnic on a blanket in the park and I'm sipping my fizzy drink and I see this sparkly thing around the straw at the bottom of the bottle," she said, her eyes getting all misty thinking of it. "I couldn't believe it."

"I'm so happy for you," I said.

"You'll be my bridesmaid, right?" She popped her eyebrows up in question.

I rolled my eyes. "Like I would have it any other way, you silly goose."

She filled me in on her adventures as we ordered and ate, laughing and chatting. Then I filled her in on my disaster of a life and the whole situation with the shop and Jack, lowering my voice considerably when I got to the part of my criminal endeavours.

"Oh, Nora. That's terrible." Her shoulders fell. "I'm so sorry you're going through all of that."

I shrugged. "These things happen I suppose."

"Jack sounds like quite the toad. I had no idea. You made him sound so perfect in your letters." She huffed. "Cal always spoke highly of him when they volunteered together."

"It turns out Jack is not the chap he pretends to be," I said, releasing a long exhale. "Just another spoiled rich boy out to ruin lives for fun."

She leaned forward and grinned. "Shall we go throw eggs at his house?"

"Not eggs. They're too precious," I said before adopting my best BBC accent. "Don't you know there's a war on?"

Maisie giggled and sat back in her seat with a sigh. "This bloody war."

I nodded in agreement. "It's all so stupid and pointless." I glanced at her. "Except for your fantastic job. That's truly the only good thing about it."

"It won't last forever though," she said. "Women will be conscripted. You don't need to encourage women to sign up for war work when it's mandatory."

"Surely the Ministry will find something else for you to do," I said. "Some other kind of photography, I mean."

"I certainly hope so," she said with a half smile. "I've got a wedding to pay for."

The next morning I practically bounded down the stairs as the smell of toast, eggs, tomatoes, and sausages filled my nostrils. I'd missed my breakfasts with my aunt, uncle, and cousin while I was away. Ginger gave a friendly bark in greeting, and I picked her up in one hand and nuzzled the top of her head.

"She missed you," Marvin said as I put her back down. "She went in your room a bunch of times and whined."

"Oh! That's so sweet," I cooed, my arm around Marvin's shoulder, squishing him. "And what about you?"

"He also went in your room and whined," Harry said flatly, the tiniest hint of a smirk on his lips.

Marvin wrinkled his nose. "I didn't!"

I kissed the top of his head as he wriggled out of my grasp and sat across from me at the table, digging into his full breakfast as I poured my tea and took the first warm sip.

"It's so nice to have you back at our table," Gloria said, giving my hand a quick squeeze as she took her seat.

I beamed and nodded. "It is." I put a forkful of food in my mouth and let it melt for a moment, savouring the tastes and smells and textures of being home again.

As we neared the end of the meal, Harry cleared his throat from behind his newspaper. "Nora, do you care to explain how you paid for this?"

He set down his paper and gestured to a half-page advertisement featuring a fashion plate-style drawing of Elsie Foster-Quinn, posing in the dress I made for her, and "Archer Fashion & Tailoring" in big letters next to it.

"What on earth…?" I grabbed the newspaper, my eyes widening.

The address of the business was there, right below a big endorsement from Elsie.

"Nora Archer isn't just a seamstress, she's an artist and a genius," I read out loud. "She took one of my old, unloved dresses and gave it a complete overhaul, turning it into a modern and chic couture gown worthy of a Parisian fashion house."

I looked up at Gloria. "I could never afford this." I looked back down at the page. "I don't understand."

Gloria picked up the last piece of toast on my plate and handed it to me, giving me a pat on the shoulder. "You may want to get to work early this morning, dear."

Cramming the toast in my mouth, I nodded and ran upstairs to finish getting ready for the day, leaving a trail of crumbs in my wake.

twenty-six

JACK

———※———

"Your mother tells me you've found a new flat."

Besides grumbling "morning" at one another fifteen minutes beforehand, the conversation between my stepfather and I at the breakfast table was entirely silent. Mum and Elsie were off at some fundraising breakfast event.

It felt like another world compared to breakfasting with the Sampsons.

"Yes," I said. "I got a good deal on it since it was bombed in the spring and they are still repairing part of it."

Father sipped his black coffee. "I respect your ambition in wanting to stand on your own two feet. It's an admirable trait."

That was the nicest thing that man had ever said to me in my entire life. I actually straightened in my chair at his words.

He cleared his throat and set his coffee down, holding his hands on the table. "Just because Archie is out of danger for the moment, that doesn't mean you shouldn't or can't have a future with the business. You could still be an asset to the valuable work we do."

I tilted my head slightly. The statement was simply too absurd.

"How could that possibly be true?"

Father's brow furrowed. "You seem very capable and organized."

"Well, um, thank you," I said, thrown by this level of warmth—yes, that was *warmth* for him. "However, I've signed on to teach at Highgate Grammar for another two terms."

I heard him release a breath through his flared nostrils like an angry bull.

"As it turns out, I might be better at teaching than I once thought." I beamed. "I actually miss it now."

"I see." His mouth became a tight line.

"We both know Archie will be much better for the job than I would ever be," I said. "If there are any additional positions that need to be filled at the company you had in mind for me, I'm sure you will have plenty of qualified applicants."

"What about your financial future? You can't live on a teacher's salary—"

"I'll manage. Lots of people do. I don't need—" My gaze landed on the chandelier hanging above the long table between us. "—all of this. But I *do* need to live a life I want." A smile tugged on the corner of my mouth. "Or what else is the point?"

Five o'clock could not come fast enough.

I found myself, once again, in St. Martin's Gardens in Camden, this time tapping my foot against the ground as I sat on a bench, checking my watch every twenty-five seconds or so. Frantic butterflies panicked in my stomach and yet, in my heart, I knew I was doing the right thing, no matter how it ended.

With ten minutes to spare, I headed for Cider Lane, my hands in my trouser pockets. As I strolled, my eyes wandered the buildings along those unfamiliar streets. Many were patched up or recently fixed, fresh paint brushed along the edges of the old. There hadn't been a bombing in over three months. Although London had a long way to go before reaching her former glory, the gashes left by the Nazis were slowly getting filled, covered and cleaned up—as much as was possible when building supplies were scarce.

A wave of nerves washed over me again as I spotted the sign over Nora's shop. I noticed she finally had the time to repaint the sign, likely during her recent drought of work. It was done by hand, probably by Nora herself, with elegant curves and flourishes in the letters. She loved and treasured her shop and her work—that was evident in the care she took with each letter, her brush only slipping in a few spots.

I sidled up to the front window, leaning my shoulder against the building, and peering inside. Nora had a white pencil tucked behind her ear as she rushed from one side of her counter to the other, her eyes glued to the garment spread out in front of her. She plucked a few pins from the cushion strapped to her wrist and slipped them into place before drumming her fingers against the counter as she considered the piece. She grabbed her large scissors from a nearby jar of tools and swept around to the other side of the counter, sliding her scissors under the fabric and cutting along a line marked in white.

I could have waved my arms and she wouldn't have noticed me.

Instead, I tried the door handle and was surprised to find it unlocked, the sign still reading "Open," even though it was after five by then.

"We're actually closed. Sorry," she said, not even looking up right away. When she did, she froze, her scissors still. "Oh. Hi."

I smiled and leaned against the wall of her shop, watching as she went back to work.

"I was so busy today." She kept her eyes on her work as she spoke, focusing as she cut. "I assume I have you to thank for that advertisement in the newspaper."

"Perhaps," I said.

She glanced up at me only briefly before lowering her eyes again. "You didn't have to do that. I know you hate asking your parents for money."

"I didn't, actually," I said. "My mother and sister paid for it."

Nora lifted an eyebrow, stopping again.

"Consider it a thank-you gift for not giving their names to the police," I said. "I know it was your way of protecting me as well, and I'm grateful."

"Ah." She took a moment to finish cutting the fabric to look back at me, reluctantly meeting my gaze. "And what about Elsie's glowing testimonial? How did you persuade her to put her name to that?"

I chuckled and rubbed the back of my neck. "Well, in a few days from now, Elsie and I are traveling to Cambridge. Since I still have access to their archives, and since I'm still in touch with several professors there, I'm going to show her a first edition Jane Austen we have as well as a number of letters written to her sister."

Nora's eyes widened. "Really? Won't you get in trouble for taking advantage of your position like that?"

"It's alright. As long as Elsie wears gloves and doesn't sneeze on them, we should be fine."

Her mouth curved into a shy smile, one she didn't show very often. Nora was far more likely to grin widely and enthusiastically and laugh loudly—I loved her boisterous laugh. But her sheepish smile, that was something else altogether. Her eyes warmed and her cheeks tinted pink. There was a tender glow to her entire face that made me want to hold her so tight and never let her go.

Nora slowly moved around the counter, stopping to lock the door and turn the sign in the window. She stood in front of me, her arms wrapped around herself and watched me expectantly.

"I know why you sold the stockings in the first place," I said. "I wish you'd told me."

She shook her head. "I couldn't. It wasn't my secret to tell."

"I know you have a hard time trusting. I will keep trying to earn that trust. I don't know if I'll ever make it up to you but I will keep trying," I said, "if you'll let me."

She studied my face a long while and lowered her eyes again.

"That night we met, I had my suspicions I might fall in love with you. But now I know for certain I will love nobody but you forever. Ending things with you…" I winced. "You know, I would feel a lot more comfortable if you weren't wielding an enormous pair of scissors right now."

She laughed aloud, and I was surprised to see the glint of tears in her eyes. "But I still might want to stab you."

"I would really prefer you didn't, even though I probably deserve it."

She gave a little nod and slid the scissors onto the counter behind her before approaching me. "Say it again."

"That I deserve to be stabbed with enormous scissors?"

"No," she said, her eyes softening. "The other thing."

"That I love you? That one?"

"Yes, that one."

I brightened as I stepped closer to her, lowering my lips to her cheek. "I love you." Lightly dragging my mouth down, I kissed her jaw. "I love you." I pressed a kiss to her neck. "I love you." I breathed the words, "I love you," into her mouth once again before grazing my lips against hers. She gave a breathy sigh and kissed me back, and my whole body hummed with pure elation.

Nora grabbed my collar and pulled me closer, our kiss quickly becoming heated and eager. I buried my fingers in her hair as her fingertips ran along my back, her body warm and snug against my chest.

"I love you," she whispered into my neck, nuzzling her nose against my jaw.

Another jolt of incandescent joy ran through me at the sound of those words, and I felt myself positively glowing as she pulled me in for another fervent kiss.

I knew our life together would never be without its challenges. But I trusted the fabric that held us together could always be mended, stitched up, and made good as new again.

epilogue

<h1 style="text-align:center">Nora</h1>

———◆———

"I swear," I said, squeezing between my sewing machine table and a shelf, "this shop used to be bigger." I gave my round, pregnant belly an affectionate pat and slowly lowered myself into my chair.

Irene giggled from her place behind her sewing desk. "I think if you can't actually reach your sewing machine anymore, it might be time to stop working."

"Don't be silly," I scoffed. "I worked until I gave birth the last two times."

"Yes, I recall," Irene said. "I nearly had to act as midwife right here in the shop for the last one, remember?"

"Oh. Right."

My water had broken right there in the shop two years before and Irene rode in the ambulance to the hospital with me as I screamed and gripped her hand. The baby was rather impatient, and I thought Jack might not make it in time. Baby Maisie Gloria Parker was born an hour later, cherry red and wailing, only minutes after Jack arrived.

"I still have a month to go," I said. "Besides, I just finished sewing this frock last night. I am *not* going to ruin it. The fabric was far too expensive for that."

"Lucky you for having so much control." Irene smirked and tied off a knot on the garment she was working on.

Irene's situation eventually got a little easier when her husband stopped drinking and began opening up to her about the horrors he witnessed on the battlefield. He slept better, their bond strengthened, and he was able to get a job working on the docks with Irene's brother. Irene's mother's health improved when they were able to move away from their flat to somewhere nicer, and she helped to take care of the little ones while Irene worked with me.

"I love that dress by the way," Irene said. "It's so bright and pretty."

I smoothed down the bountiful skirt and smiled down at the playful rose print. "Thank you." Wistfully, I thought back to the days of Archer Fashion & Tailoring, my beloved little shop in Camden. "I never imagined styles would change so much in a decade."

The New Look took over once the war ended and suddenly every fashionable woman had a narrow, nipped waist and full skirt. Britain didn't make replicating the modern style easy since they still had their utility scheme going, limiting designers to so many buttons, pockets, yards of fabric and stitching, et cetera. It was a challenge.

But I always loved a challenge.

Jack and I were both focused on our careers and decided to wait a few years before starting a family. My tailoring business was still successful although fabric became harder to come by as the years progressed. Rationing of clothes and food became stricter. For about a year, I taught Make Do and Mend sewing classes on Wednesday evenings, and the students and I exchanged tips and tricks for reusing different materials and saving what we could. Soon before the birth of our son, David John Parker, I closed my shop and dedicated myself one hundred percent to motherhood.

For all of about two months.

While my perfect boy slept peacefully in his crib, I sketched designs for outfits I wanted to sew for myself that would be comfortable and flattering while I lost the baby weight. Then I had friends and some old clients contacting me about clothes and before I knew it, I was hanging a sign over the door of a new business: Nora Parker. My own couturier shop. If it weren't for our full-time housekeeper and Gloria coming on as a nanny, I don't know how I would have made it work.

The door of my shop creaked open as Jack let himself in, his leather satchel over his shoulder. I beamed at him, my handsome husband, now donning a few distinguished white hairs at his temples.

Irene waved. "If you're here, that must mean I'm late for my train home." She kissed my cheek and headed out for the day.

Jack plopped down in Irene's vacated chair. "How are you feeling?"

I let out a little laugh. "I keep telling everyone I'm fine, yet nobody seems to believe me." I rolled one of my shoulders and before I could ask him to rub it for me, Jack was on his feet with his thumbs pressed into the sore flesh.

I sighed. "Thank you, love."

Jack kept his teaching job until the end of the war. Although he would never admit it, he was sad to leave his young pupils behind, having grown to love their shenanigans as well as their young and inquisitive minds. He went back to Cambridge to be a researcher, but not being able to see one another except on weekends put a strain on our relationship. He also didn't find it as fulfilling as he once did. He soon found a job as a researcher at King's College in London. Surprising everyone he knew Jack landed a position as an assistant professor at King's, and he was back in front of eager students again. And he'd never looked happier.

Our home was a busy one, full of books, fashion sketches, children's toys, and laughter. And more love and joy than I could have ever imagined.

what about his letters?

What exactly did those lost letters from Jack to Nora say?
Sign up at **jilly.ca/letters-freebie** to find out.

about the next homefront hearts book

Bravery and fortitude on the English homefront endure in this lighthearted, enemies-to-lovers WWII romance, perfect for fans of *The Wartime Matchmakers* and *Dear Mrs. Bird*.

Expecting a relaxing getaway at her family's summer estate, pampered socialite Elsie Foster-Quinn signs up for the Women's Land Army. When she ends up at a Somerset dairy farm instead, Elsie immediately butts heads with the grumpy farmer she now works for. Being a land girl in a small town is far more than the city girl bargained for.

Ben Grainger hates asking for help. When two land girls unexpectedly arrive on his farm, he quickly learns he can't simply make them go away. He finds amusement in tormenting Elsie whose privileged life certainly didn't prepare her for farm life. However, nothing could have prepared Ben for the feelings that suddenly emerge whenever the haughty little princess is near.

Why can't he keep his eyes off her? And why can't she stop thinking about him? Opposites attract—but is it true love?

Between the Germans bombing nearby Bath and a deadly disease rampaging through local farms, Ben and Elsie's trust in each other is put to the ultimate test.

THE LAND GIRL ON LILY ROAD, the final novel in the Homefront Hearts WWII romance trilogy, will be released on March 4, 2024.

Learn more at jilly.ca/homefront-hearts

acknowledgements

Thank you so much for reading *The Seamstress on Cider Lane*.

If you enjoyed this book, I would appreciate it if you could take a few minutes and leave a review on whatever book retailer you purchased from.
Reviews are the easiest way to support authors.

If you would like to hear from me and get subscriber-only exclusives, sign up to my monthly newsletter: **jilly.ca/subscribe**

Thank you to Colby, Mom, the rest of my family, Colleen, Geoff, and my lovely readers.

Made in United States
Cleveland, OH
03 February 2025

14027655R00109